M. E. M. (Mollie Evelyn Moore) Davis

Under the Man-fig

M. E. M. (Mollie Evelyn Moore) Davis

Under the Man-fig

ISBN/EAN: 9783742894410

Manufactured in Europe, USA, Canada, Australia, Japa

Cover: Foto ©Andreas Hilbeck / pixelio.de

Manufactured and distributed by brebook publishing software
(www.brebook.com)

M. E. M. (Mollie Evelyn Moore) Davis

Under the Man-fig

UNDER THE MAN-FIG

BY

M. E. M. DAVIS

AUTHOR OF "IN WAR TIMES AT LA ROSE BLANCHE," "MINDING THE GAP," ETC., ETC.

BOSTON AND NEW YORK
HOUGHTON, MIFFLIN AND COMPANY
The Riverside Press, Cambridge
1895

CONTENTS

UNDER THE MAN-FIG.

PROLOGUE.

THE TOWN AND THE RIVER.

THE name of the River is *Los Brazos de Dios*, which is to say, The Arms of God.

The bed of it is very deep; and the color of the water — when it creeps sluggishly along between its banks, so shallow in places that the blue heron may wade it without wetting his knees — is the color of tarnished brass. But when it comes roaring down from the far-away Redlands, a solid foam-crested wall, leaping upward a foot a minute, and spreading death and destruction into the out-lying lowlands, then it is as red as spilled blood.

On its banks, more than a century and a half ago, a handful of barefoot Franciscan friars, who had prayed and fought their way across the country from Mexico, founded the Presidio of St. Jago, and corralled within the boundary walls a flock of *Yndios redu-cidos.*

There were the stately church, cloistered and towered and rose-windowed, — a curious flower of architecture abloom in the savage wilderness, — and the block-house with its narrow loopholes, and the hut into which the Indian women were thrust at night under lock and key.

The mighty forest and open prairies around teemed with Yndios bravos, who hated the burly, cassocked, fighting monks, and their own Christianized tribesmen.

These came, in number like the leaves of the live-oak, to hurl themselves against the Presidio. And, after many days of hard fighting, the single friar who remained alive turned his eyes away from the demolished church, and, under cover of smoke from the burning block-house, led the remnant of Yndios reducidos (who because they had learned to pray had not forgotten how to fight) out of the inclosure by a little pos-tern-gate, and down the steep bank to the yellow thread of the River below.

Midway of the stream — thridding the ankle-deep water — they were, before the red devils above discovered their flight. The demoniac yell from a thousand throats pushed them like a battering-ram up the opposite bank, whence, looking back, they saw the bed of the River Tockonhono swarming with their foes. Then the Yndios reducidos opened their lips and began to chant the death-song of the Nainis; and the friar, lifting his hand, commended their souls and his own to the God who gives and who takes away.

But, lo, a miracle.

Even as the waves of the Red Sea — opened by the rod of Moses for the passage of his people — closed upon Pharaoh and his host, so, with the hoarse roar of a wild beast springing upon his prey, the foam-crested wall of water fell upon the Yndios bravos, and not a warrior of them all came forth from the river-bed but as a bruised and beaten corpse.

So the friar, falling on his knees, gave thanks. And the River, which was the Tockonhono, became from that day Los Brazos de Dios, which is to say, The Arms of God.

Such is the legend of the River.

.   .   .   .

The town is on the River. It was built

there nearly a hundred years after the forgotten Presidio of St. Jago.

It was reckoned once a centre of luxury and refinement. But that was during the epoch of the short-lived republic, and before the time of June Badgett.

It has changed but little, however, since the days when June and his cronies foregathered, gossiping, under the Man-Fig.

The gray weather-beaten old stores fronting the River drowse in the mellow sunshine like contented old folks who could, if they would, wake up and babble of past glories with the best.

The shadows of the great live-oaks lie athwart the by-streets, and above them rise the roofs of the same many-galleried aristocratic old mansions that shelter later generations of the same aristocratic old families.

The ferryman — it is always a Hopson, the office is hereditary — still shuffles down the bank after he has been called a dozen or so times, and pulls the shackly ferry-boat across the river. You can hear the pulley creaking its way along the rope half-way to the railroad station, which is at the edge of a cotton-patch on the other side of the river. The train, as in the year of our Lord eighteen hundred and fifty-seven (when the story begins), lumbers in and out at uncertain hours. If you are intending to leave, and should be delayed, it will wait for you a reasonable length of time, — say three quarters of an hour; though, unless you are acquainted with its vagaries, you may be startled into undue haste by the wild shrieks with which the locomotive beguiles its tarrying.

The warehouse has not sloughed a shingle from its roof in all these years, nor lost a brick of its sturdy old walls.

The boats sailing the River — which goes Gulf-ward, now hesitating and reluctant, now thundering down in headlong haste, whipping its red waves into spume — may be new, but they look, with their black hulls and patched sails, like the boats which sailed the River forty years ago.

The townsmen still sit about under the store-sheds, — standing up, hat in hand, every mother's son of 'em, when a woman, young or old, homely or beautiful, chances to pass, — comfortably minding each other's business, and free, neighbor to neighbor, of pocket as of tongue.

Girls, slim and supple in their white

gowns, flit of summer afternoons through the purpling shadows; and the sound of their voices is like the cooing of young pigeons.

In short, the old town — the lovablest, old-timiest, easy-goingest old town that ever was — sits there by the River, hugging its traditions, and hoarding its stories, of which it has enough to make a new Thousand and One Nights.

Under the Man-Fig is one of these.

I.

THE COURT IN SESSION.

"Van Herrin'! Well, I reckon! I'd know his hide ef I saw it in a tan-yard!"

The speaker — a short thick-set man, with a broad face, red bristly beard and small twinkling eyes — slapped his hand against his thigh, and looked somewhat defiantly around upon his auditors.

"Oh, I did n't mean to doubt ye, June," said one of these in an aggressively skeptical tone, "but ef it was night-time" —

"It was betwix' nine an' ten o'clock at night," interrupted the first speaker, with emphasis. "I 'd been down to Sam Billups's after a load o' watermelons, an' I was a-drivin' kinder slow (my team bein' blowed), an' jis' as I got to the turn o' the road beyan Roseneath, I saw a man step out on the side-gall'ry, through one of them long winders. He stood a minit ag'ins' the light "—

"You could n't o' reco'nized nobody's face on Miss Thornham's side-gall'ry fum that turn o' the road, June Badgett," put in his opponent doggedly.

"Hold your jaw, Rufe Drennon," replied the man Badgett. "Gentlemen," he continued, turning his back on the doubter and addressing the others, "I saw a man come out'n one of them long winders an' stan' a minit on the side-gall'ry. Then he jumped down an' come acrost Miss Elinor's rose-garden; an' as I drove past, he opened the gate an' come out. The moon was as bright as day. I don't b'lieve he saw me at all. He was lookin' straight ahead of him, an' his eyes bugged out like a fire-beetle's. But I saw *him* plain enough. He went down the road todes his own house. An' I wish my Maker may strike me stone dead ef that man wa'n't Van Herrin'!"

"You 've been a-tellin' o' that tale studdy fer the las' three weeks," said Drennon, after a short pause, during which they all ruminated silently on the threadbare but still exciting story. "'N ef you 're so dead shore that Van Heerin' took 'em, why 'nt you"—

"I ain't shore," interrupted Badgett again, thrusting his hands into his pockets and settling back against the fence. "All I know is, I saw Van Herrin' with my own eyes, come out'n Miss Thornham's side-gate three weeks ago to-night."

The men who composed the small group were lounging in the shade of an enormous fig-tree, whose gnarled and knobby branches overhung one corner of an abandoned dooryard. This landmark — older, some said, than the town of Thornham itself — was known as the Man-Fig. It had long ceased to bear the luscious fruit which the oldest inhabitant — June Badgett's father — remembered to have gathered, surreptitiously, when a boy. But it continued to thrive in a scraggy sort of way, leaning over the fence, — which served at once as a hitching-place for horses and a support for the backs of the village idlers, — and sending its sprawly roots out in every direction. The origin of its name was unknown. A dim legend survived of the murdered Spaniard whose blood had watered its infant roots, and passed into its great reddish-purple fruit. But this half-forgotten story was only recalled by the inquiry of some curious stranger, the familiar appellation making no impression upon accustomed ears. During the short winter, which brought a bleak look to the spot, nipping the banana leaves and scorching the cannæ that grew in uncultivated profusion about the deserted house in the inclosure, the open space beneath the Man-Fig was left to stray cows, or to the colts whose whinnying dams were tethered to the rotting fence. But all through the semi-tropical spring and the long hot summer, its scant shade sheltered the male contingent of the Thornham gossips. They stood about, leaning against the fence, or squatted on the ground, gravely discussing all manner of questions — from the President's last message to the ear-marks of their own hogs. More than one political campaign had been planned under the Man-Fig; and, truth to tell, more than one reputation laid on the rack.

The stillness which succeeded June Badgett's last remark was broken by the shrill whistle of a locomotive. There was a perfunctory movement under the Man-Fig. Dud Welsh stood up and looked across the river at the crowd running toward the little station, and at the ferryman descending, on the hither side, the deep cut in the bank, to where the ferry-boat was fastened.

"I might sell some o' them watermelons over at the *dee*-po'," remarked Badgett tentatively, lifting a lazy elbow toward his wagon, which stood a few yards away, its deep bed loaded with green, glistening, round-bellied melons, "but it's too durned hot. I ain't goin' acrost."

A sigh of relief passed through the squad. The wide street which ran along the river-bank lay hot and dusty in the quivering noontide heat. The stores and offices facing it were apparently deserted; though from time to time, when a plantation team crawled in and stopped, a shirt-sleeved clerk came languidly out to take an order; or a booted and spurred horseman, jingling up, passed the time of day with the invisible proprietor dozing on his chair within. At Addington's warehouse, hunched against the bluff above the ferry, there were signs of life. A heavy bolt fell with a clang, the wooden doors swung open, a man appeared on the thresh-old, gesticulating, and shouting orders into space, and a dozen stalwart half-naked ne-groes swarmed suddenly down the bank and leaped upon the ferry-boat as it drew away from the shore.

"I reckon Jack Addington's lookin' fer some freight," said Tuke Chancellor, gazing after them. "Well, boys, it's too late to

git over now. Anyhow, 't ain't wuth the
trouble. She's gittin' plum rickety."

The houses composing the town of Thornham — buried in vines and shrubbery, and
shaded by mighty and magnificent live-oaks
— followed in single file the curves of the
river, — now low and sullen-looking between
its high banks. The town in general had
an old and worn-out look, though not a half-
century had gone by since the underbrush
was cleared from its site, and barely a quarter since Steven Thornham built the first
brick house — a stately mansion a stone's-
throw or so from the Man-Fig — and turned
his attention to ousting Mexican authority
from the vast region of country then beginning to be known as Texas. But it had
had its day in the mean time, the placid little town! Epauleted officers had lounged
along its muddy sidewalks; couriers had
galloped in and out with sealed dispatches;
Santa Anna, a prisoner of war, had strutted
its single street. There, the first constitu-
tional government had been inaugurated;
and the president of the young republic
had there taken his oath of office. The
after-glow of that gay and courtly time still
lingered about the aristocratic town houses

and the luxurious plantation homes that lined the downward-sweeping river on either side to within sound of the beating Gulf-surge. Later stories there were, too, of silent craft that had crept stealthily up the stream to discharge human freight, akin in color to the midnight shadows that hung about the stoop-shouldered warehouse, and slipped as stealthily back into the Gulf and thence toward the coast of Guinea.

Then came the puff of the first locomotive-engine. The wonder of this had not yet died away. "She" was due once a day, and — sometimes several moments earlier, oftener an hour or more later, than the schedule time — the train came snorting noisily in, jolting and jostling the infrequent passengers. The station, separated from Thornham proper by the river, presented at such times a busy and animated appearance. Rarely indeed did man or boy, — though the spectacle entailed a hurried rush to the ferry and a run up the steep bank on the opposite side, — rarely did a Thornhamer miss the sight of the incoming or outgoing of the lumbering engine, and its single dingy comfortless coach.

"I wonder ef she's fetched any passengers," said Jimmy Hopson, the youngest of the Man-Fig conclave, secretly longing, yet ashamed to bolt away at the last moment to see "her" uncoupled and side-tracked for the night.

"Who is that with Pete Newall?" demanded Badgett abruptly, peering out from under the brim of his straw hat.

A light buggy drawn by a gaunt gray horse came up the river-bank from the ferry and glanced by, throwing the dust in their faces as it passed. It was driven by a large clean-shaven man with keen gray eyes and a kindly mouth; his somewhat careless dress was in accord with the unkempt look of the vehicle and harness, and the rough coat of the raw-boned but swift horse. His companion — a man near his own age, thirty-five years or thereabout — offered a striking contrast in manner and appearance. His dark neat traveling-suit was faultless in cut and fit. He sat erect, with his gloved hands resting upon his knees. Everything about his slender and elegant person bespoke a high-bred and somewhat haughty repose. His blue eyes were hard and cold; a drooping mustache concealed his mouth, but not the firm, somewhat projecting chin. He seemed to ignore the presence of his escort, and he looked neither to right nor left as they whirled along the dusty highway.

"I b'lieve in my soul it's Johnny Thornham!" exclaimed Badgett, jumping to his feet and staring after the buggy. "I ain't seen him sence he left here nigh twenty years ago. But he's got the same biggaty look he was born with; and — yes! they've turned into Miss Elinor's big gate."

.   .   .   .

"Will you come first to my office? or shall I drive you to the hotel, Jo — Mr. Thornham?" Newall asked with his foot on the step of the buggy. He had to repeat his question as he seated himself beside the newcomer and picked up the reins; for the engine was shrieking and backing amid the delighted clamor of the crowd about the platform.

"Neither, thank you, Mr. Newall," replied his guest courteously; "I will go at once to Roseneath, if you please."

Hardly a word further was exchanged between the two men until they turned in at the large iron gate at Roseneath and drove slowly around the circular oak-shaded carriage-way to the house.

"The grounds seem much smaller than I remember them," Thornham said, turning upon the broad gallery and looking about him with something like a contemptuous sneer.

"It is a fine old place," retorted his companion a little hotly; then, as if ashamed of his haste, he added quietly, "Miss Thornham was very fond of it."

"So was my mother." The stranger said this almost under his breath, following the lawyer down the wide hall and into the large old-fashioned parlor.

Here Newall seated himself by an open window, turning his head with innate delicacy while Thornham walked about the well-remembered room, pausing now and then to touch, with a restless finger, a yellowed book, or a dust-covered ornament. The sunlight streaming in through the windows fell full upon the two portraits over the mantel. He glanced for a second at the stern pictured face of his father; his own face hardened into a likeness of it, and a bitter smile curved his thin lips. But his eyes softened as he turned to the other portrait. He rested his arm on the mantel and gazed long and musingly upon it.

It seemed but yesterday! The cold, selfish, rich, prosperous man of the world felt himself trembling once more under the harsh denunciatory sentence of that Steven Thornham, of whom it was said that he broke, or bent, everything that came to his hand; he felt again, warm upon his forehead, his mother's tears.

"Let us come to business, Mr. Newall," he said brusquely, straightening himself and passing his gloved hand across his eyes.

He led the way himself, and as if instinctively, into a small room which opened upon a side - gallery. It overlooked the rose-garden, and had been his mother's morning - room. It was absolutely unchanged in all these years! There was the low chintz-covered lounge with its high-piled pillows; the claw-footed table; the spider-legged secretary; the brass-bound work-stand with the silver sewing - bird perched upon its edge, — even the familiar little dog-eared Thomas-à-Kempis, open and face downward on the embroidered hassock!

A large Newfoundland dog lying on a rug alongside the couch looked up with a questioning growl as they entered, then arose and walked over to where Thornham stood, and laid a shaggy head against his knee. He shrugged his shoulders as if shaking off an importunate sentiment, and seated himself, motioning the lawyer to a chair.

"You will tell me the particulars of my sister's death," he began, giving an impatient push to the dog, which nevertheless continued to nestle affectionately against him. "You will remember, as I have already written you, that I have heard next to nothing of her since my mother died, ten years ago. In fact," he added, "I can scarcely realize her at all. She was, you know, some years younger than I; and I was, myself, little more than a boy when I went away."

"Yes," assented the lawyer, "I know. Well, after your father's death, your mother " —

"It is not necessary to speak of my mother," interrupted Thornham coldly. "Confine yourself, if you please, to my sister Elinor and her affairs."

"Just after your — her — mother died," continued Newall, stammering a little, but recovering himself, "Miss Elinor fell into delicate health."

"There had been some sort of love-affair, had there not?" asked his listener, apparently without much interest, for his eyes were wandering abstractedly about his mother's sitting-room.

"Yes," — the lawyer flushed a little, — "there had been a love-affair. Miss Elinor — that is — Miss Thornham — was engaged for a couple of years to her second cousin, Vanborough Herring. Do you remember him?"

"No," returned Thornham listlessly. "I never saw him. He came to Thornham after I left. So he was the man. What became of him?"

"The engagement was broken off — no one ever knew why — just after your — after Mrs. Thornham died. Herring went away — to Kentucky, I think; and a year later he came back, bringing a wife with him."

Thornham looked up as if suddenly aroused. A dark red spot showed for a second on either cheek, and his eyes flashed. But he did not speak.

"He has continued to live here in Thornham. He belongs to the poorer branch of

the Vanborough - Thornhams. He has a
large family. He is a lawyer; hardwork-
ing enough, but he has never seemed to
make any headway. She — she was very
fond of him."

Newall uttered these sentences in a jerky
sort of way, singularly different from the
professional tone he had hitherto used.

Thornham looked at him a moment in
silence ; then, as if dismissing Vanborough
Herring from the conversation, he inquired : "Was my sister's illness a long
one ? "

" Yes, and no," Newall returned. "During the ten years that she lived here alone
after your — for ten years she was subject,
at intervals, to sudden and painful attacks,
— some trouble with the heart, I believe ;
and in one of these paroxysms she finally
died. But much of the time she was well ;
and though leading a quiet and almost se-
cluded life, she took a vivid interest in
everything that went on here in Thornham,
as well as in the outside world. Hers was
a most lovely character. She was very
beautiful. And so young to die ! She was
barely thirty, you know."

There was a tremor in his voice which did

not escape his hearer, and his own tone was less hard when he spoke, after a short pause : —

"She must have been very like my mother! Who was with her when she died?"

"No one. She died, in this room, on yonder couch, three weeks ago to-night, — alone. Not neglected, oh, no!" — seeing the wrathful frown on the face before him, — "not uncared for! She had been slightly ailing for some days, and unable to take her accustomed drive. She seemed depressed, too, and unusually restless. She came to this room — she was, in fact, carried, in the arms of one of her servants, as I understand — late that afternoon ; and here Doctor Alsbury saw her soon after nightfall. She was weak and nervous, but quite free of pain. Mrs. Hopson — you remember Aunt Patty Hopson? She was your mo — Mrs. Thornham's housekeeper before you were born." Thornham nodded. "Aunt Patty and her maid were with her. But when the doctor had taken his leave, she sent them both away, desiring, as she often did, to be alone. She was lying upon the lounge, with the small table beside her, the bell within reach of her hand. Mrs. Hopson went into the dining-room, with the maid, and remained there, superintending some household matters. Nearly two hours passed. The night was warm and still, the house very quiet. Aunt Patty had just observed to the maid that Miss Elinor had probably dropped asleep, when Magnus, the old Newfoundland there, who was lying at her feet, got up, as if suddenly aroused, and came down the hall in this direction. The girl called to him softly, fearful lest he should disturb her mistress, but he passed on, and a moment later they were startled by a piteous howl which rang through the silent house. They ran, frightened, into the room. The dog was leaping distractedly against the couch, where his mistress was lying, white and motionless, apparently in a heavy swoon. The doctor, hastily summoned, found life extinct. Death had come to her — painlessly, he said — in one of those spasms of the heart to which she was subject. She had been dead perhaps half an hour."

The speaker's voice died away in something like a smothered sob. The dog, at mention of his name, had lifted his great head and fixed his intelligent eyes upon Thornham's face. He now walked over to the couch and stood there whining softly. There was a moment of pained silence.

Thornham half arose, but reseated himself, arrested by a fleeting expression which crossed his companion's face.

"There is something more," he said quietly; "go on."

Newall looked up surprised; he flushed a little and moved uneasily in his chair.

"Yes," he admitted, dropping his eyes, "there is something I ought to tell you, but "—

"Well?" demanded Thornham, as he hesitated.

The lawyer cleared his throat and proceeded. "About the time the lamps were brought in that night, she asked Aunt Patty to bring her a box from her jewel-case. It contained, I am told, a diamond necklet of great beauty and value "—

"I have never heard of it," Thornham said, answering a look in the speaker's eyes; "but, then, I know nothing whatever of my sister's life, or her possessions."

"She held the box in her hand during the doctor's visit. No one is known to have entered the room afterward; but when the alarm and excitement over her sudden death had somewhat subsided, Mrs. Hopson remembered the box and desired to return it to the casket. It had disappeared. It was then noticed that one of the windows — the one next you there — opening upon the side-gallery, which was closed when Aunt Patty and the maid left the room — was standing open. There were heavy footprints in the rose-bed beneath the gallery, and leading off into the rose-garden, showing that some one had jumped down and passed across to the gate."

" Who is suspected ? " demanded Thornham, with keen interest.

The lawyer's voice dropped to a shamed whisper. "No one is known to have entered the house, but Herring was seen coming out of this window about three quarters of an hour after Mrs. Hopson quitted the room."

" A Vanborough!   Impossible!" cried Thornham angrily.

A look of relief came into Newall's eyes.

" I felt bound to mention this circumstance," he said, " but I myself believe Vanborough Herring incapable of " —

Thornham was not listening. He got up

and made two or three turns about the small room, the dog following at his heels.

"Investigate it," he said sharply at length, pausing before his companion. "Investigate it," he repeated, interrupting a hurried protest. "If a Vanborough can rob a dead woman, by God! and a woman he has jilted, he ought to suffer for it! Look into it at once and prosecute if necessary; spare no expense." He brought his fist down on the small table as he spoke. The tray of glasses there quivered, filling the room with their crystalline tinkle.

"Very well, sir," said Newall briefly.

They passed into the hall. "That rattle-trap of a train leaves, I believe, at ten o'clock to-morrow morning?" Thornham asked.

"You surely do not think of returning so soon," said the lawyer astonished. "I thought" —

"I have important business elsewhere," interrupted Thornham again. "Or, rather," he continued, with a short unmusical laugh, — "in God's name, what have I to do with the town of Thornham or its people! I wish my mother's portrait forwarded as soon as possible to my address in New Orleans.

And my sister's," he added as an after-thought. "I will advise you as to what disposition to make of the family belongings and my sister's private property. As to the house and grounds, sell at once. I have no sentiment about the place. I sometimes wish I had kept Fair View, the plantation down the river, where my mother used to go with me during my vacation days. But I sold that when it came into my possession after my father's death. Yes, sell Roseneath — at once, if possible."

" And the negroes — the house-servants? There are a good many of them. Elinor " —

" Sell them! At once! I have no use for such property. Sell it all; horses — I suppose my sister kept horses?"

" As fine a pair as ever trotted in harness," replied Newall, visibly nettled.

" Very well. Sell them all. Sell everything." He tossed a defiant glance at his father's portrait, for they were standing again in the parlor. "I leave the whole business in your hands. You will communicate at need with my lawyers in New Orleans. And now, have the goodness to drive me to a hotel. I am a little tired after my long journey."

The Newfoundland shambled down the steps behind him; and, after he was seated in the buggy, reared up to place a huge paw upon his knee.

They talked — spasmodically — of indifferent subjects as they drove back through the town, Newall secretly wondering at his companion's utter want of curiosity or interest concerning his birthplace and the people among whom his boyhood had passed.

"I suppose you are married, Mr. Newall?" The question sounded perfunctory.

"No, I'm not married," returned Newall curtly, as the buggy stopped before The President's Rest tavern, — so called because Sam Houston had slept there the night preceding his inauguration.

The afternoon shadows had lengthened, and a breeze blew up salt from the Gulf. The town was slowly awaking from its prolonged nap. Old Mr. Lusk, standing in his store door, was holding an animated conversation with Uncle Billy Duncan, in his spider-wheeled gig. Ned Cushington had come out of the "Gazette" office with a paper — moist and smelling of printers' ink — in his hand, and was reading a bit of late news to some men on a corner; his fine dark eyes were flashing with excitement. Women and girls, in groups of twos and threes, in light summer gowns, flitted about the grassy by-ways. A stentorian chorus arose from Addington's warehouse, where the negroes were piling freight.

The loafers under the Man-Fig commented idly upon the actors in this familiar panorama.

"I wish my Maker may strike me stone dead ef it ain't Johnny Thornham shore enough!" declared Badgett, breaking in upon Tuke Chancellor's description of one of Major Billy Duncan's tantrums; "an' as *vi*-grous as old Steve his-se'f!"

"Then it's high time for Van Herrin' to light out," suggested Welsh.

"Shucks!" said Drennon, standing up and stretching his long arms above his head with a grunt, "he neenter be skeered. No Thornham ain't goin' to prosecute no other Thornham."

"Bet you that load o' watermelons 'g'ins' a cob-pipe!" cried Badgett.

.　　.　　.　　.　　.　　.　　.　　.

"Unearth that d——d hound of a Vanborough, Mr. Newall," Thornham reiterated, the next morning, drawing on his gloves, after glancing over and signing the few necessary papers drawn up the night before by the lawyer. He stepped out of the dingy and disordered little office after a formal adieu, politely declining Newall's offer to drive him to the station. He walked briskly along the shaded side street, for the lawyer's office was set well back from the river in the rear of the business portion of the town. He did not so much as turn his head in the direction of the old Thornham mansion, whose steep roof and red-brick chimneys showed above the live-oaks away to the right. His busy thoughts had already leaped forward to his city life: his elegant bachelor apartments, his club, the opera, the races, the never-ending round of amusement and distraction which had become so necessary to his well-being. That his vast wealth was augmented by a small fortune was hardly compensation for the physical discomfort and the troublesome sentiment of the past twenty-four hours. In three or four days, at the farthest —

He stopped suddenly. Something warm and soft, like a rose-leaf, had touched his wrist. He looked down. A child — a little girl of seven or eight years — had put out a hand to arrest him; with the other she tugged at the latch of a large wooden gate which abutted upon the uneven plank sidewalk.

"I can't get in by myself," she said, looking gravely up at him. "Maum Betty could n't come with me. Please open it."

He glanced beyond her at the house which stood at the further end of a prim shelled walk, and he laughed aloud at the memories evoked by the sight of its porches and gables; then he dropped his eyes again upon the child, and his laugh softened to a smile. The little maid, tall, perhaps, for her years, had that look, delicate but not unhealthy, common to growing children. Her small, rather plain, oval face, with its soft outlines, was lighted by a pair of large dark eyes, whose serious expression seemed at variance with the pretty laughing mouth. The mass of reddish-brown hair which fell over her shoulders was trained, after the fashion of the time, into long loose ringlets. A certain daintiness about her person and manner bespoke gentle blood and tender care.

"What is your name, little one?" Thornham asked, with his hand on the latch.

"Olive Vanborough Herring," she answered promptly, with a proud uplifting of her firm little chin.

"Are you the daughter of Mr. Vanborough Herring?"

She nodded her head with great satisfaction. "Yes, sir. Olive Vanborough Herring," she repeated.

He pushed open the heavy gate, stooping a little as he did so. He had not dreamed of offering to kiss the child. But she put up her mouth frankly. A curious thrill passed through him as he felt upon his own the warm touch of her red lips.

She ran gayly along the flower-set walk toward the house. He swung the gate to its place, frowning. The engine over at the station was already puffing and shrieking. From where he stood he could see people hastening toward the ferry, and he heard the hurry and bustle about the warehouse, where some belated barrels were being rolled down the bank. He shook his head impatiently, muttered something under his breath, then turned and walked rapidly back toward the lawyer's office.

Newall still sat in the worn leather chair where his client had left him. His head had fallen forward on his breast, his usually jovial face was downcast, his eyes weary and troubled. "Poor Van!" he sighed. "She loved him to the last—that I know. It will be necessary for him to go away, at least until the matter blows over. For "— He sprang to his feet as a shadow darkened the door. "What is it, Mr. Thornham?" he asked confusedly. "Have you forgotten anything? Can I "—

"I cannot wait, Newall," interrupted Thornham. "I have only come back to say that I have decided not to have that robbery investigated. There is not sufficient proof to my mind. It certainly is not a matter of importance to any one except myself. Vanborough Herring is not to be disturbed. See to it, please."

"Thank you, Johnny!" cried Newall involuntarily. "Elinor loved "—

He turned aside, blushing crimson. Thornham, almost equally embarrassed, picked up a fishing-rod which was lying upon a heap of legal documents on the table, and pretended to examine it.

"So you still fish, Pete?" he said gayly, after an imperceptible pause. "Do you remember the day we upset your father's boat in the river, and how near you came to drowning because you would n't let go the string of catfish tied to the oar-lock?"

The parting hand-shake this time was warm and cordial, and Thornham hurried away to catch his train. "*Olive Vanborough!*" he murmured, as he passed the gate where he had met the clear-eyed child. It had been the maiden name of his mother — that idolized mother from whose arms he had been driven by a father's curse — the only human being he had ever loved — the sole living creature, he told himself passionately, that had ever cared whether he himself lived or died!

A succession of shrieks from the distant locomotive caused him to quicken his steps. An anxious frown lowered upon his brow. "Am I to be left another night in this beastly hole," he growled aloud.

"Neb-min', Mars Johnny," said a voice at his elbow. "Don't you be skeered. She 's gwine to wait ontell you git aboard her. She ain' in no sech hurry ez she 's mekin' out."

Thornham turned, and stared blankly at the speaker.

"Lawd, Mars Johnny, you ain' fergot

Lib!" the negro went on, catching the light traveling-bag from his hand and falling a pace or two behind him as he moved on.

"Why, Liberty!" he cried, shaking his old playfellow heartily by the hand. "Is this you?" His blue eyes lighted with genuine pleasure. "What have you been doing all these years, you rascal? Digging bait? and stealing *red-injun* peaches? and riding the horses to water, eh?"

Liberty, a gigantic, well-made, neatly-dressed *griffe*, a year or two younger than his master, drew himself up. "No, sah," he replied proudly. "I has been Miss Elinor's butler for a matter o' ten year, sah."

"Miss Elinor's butler, eh?" said Thornham, amused.

"Yes, sah. When ole Mis' died, Miss Elinor she took me from de stable an' fotch me inter de house. An' I been her butler ever sence."

"What did you do?" demanded his companion, still smiling.

"I mos'ly took keer o' Miss Elinor, sah. You see, Mars Johnny, Miss Elinor wa'n't overly strong a'ter ole Mis' died; an' she useter say nobody could'n tote her up an' down stairs like Liberty. Lawd, she wa'n't nothin' to *tote*, Miss Elinor wa'n't! Light ez a baby! No mo' 'n de same day she died, I fotch her into yo' ma's settin'-room an' laid her on de longe. An' when she look' up at me wi' dem big eyes o' hern, stidder speakin', Mars Johnny, I know'd"—

He shook his head, unable to go on. The tears streamed unheeded down his cheeks.

"Liberty," said his master abruptly, "you know everything is going to be sold, and Roseneath broken up?"

"Yes, sah," said Liberty anxiously. "I was born on de place, Mars Johnny," he added, in a wistful tone.

"I know," Thornham went on; "so was I. But I shall sell it. How would you like to come to New Orleans with me?"

The anxiety on the negro's face deepened. An appealing look came into his big dog-like eyes.

"Very well," continued his master, without disappointment. "Then you'd rather I gave you your freedom?"

"Mars Johnny," Liberty said, edging up to him and speaking in a confidential tone, "don't you do no sech foolishness ez dat. I ain' made fer no free-nigger. I has lived all my life 'long o' white folks, an' I ain' fitten to live 'long o' free-niggers. Lawd, Mars Johnny, I run away once in ole Mars's lifetime; an' I stayed down yander in de Brazos bottom 'long o' some yether runaway niggers 'bout fo' days. An' 'fo' Gawd, Mars Johnny, I was glad when I was cotch, an' fotch in! But what is de mos' consequenche is Betty. Betty is my ole 'ooman. An' Betty ain' got no use fer free-niggers!" He laughed softly.

"Who owns your wife?"

"Mars Van Herrin', sah; Betty's a lakly gal. Spry on her foot ez a sparrer. No, Mars Johnny, thanky all de same. I don't want no freedom 'dout Betty. An' Betty would'n leave her white folks not ef she was set free ter-morrer."

"Well, Lib," said his master carelessly, setting foot on the ferry-boat which had answered the negro's sonorous call, "if you do not wish to come with me, and are not willing to be set free, I suppose you will have to go on the block."

"I reckin so, Mars Johnny," Liberty returned dejectedly. "Gawd sen' dey don't sell me fur away fum Betty."

The boat slipped across the yellow stream,

the wooden pulley creaking as it moved along the heavy rope. They walked up the farther bank in silence. The train was apparently awaiting the belated passenger, for at sight of him the brakeman ran along the platform and called out cheerfully, "All right, Cap, here he comes;" and the conductor, appearing at the rear of the coach, waved his hand in friendly greeting.

Liberty stood beneath the window, chatting with his master until the train started.

"By the way," said Thornham, thrusting his hand into his pocket, "there is an old dog at Roseneath — a Newfoundland" —

"Magnus, sah! Miss Elinor's ole dog. He's been in ou' fam'ly a long time, Magnus has."

"Well, I want you to take care of that dog as long as he lives. Take him away with you when you leave Roseneath." He dropped a roll of money into the negro's hand. "Good-by, Liberty."

"All right, Mars Johnny. Thanky, Mars Johnny, thanky. Good-by, Mars Johnny."

He gazed absently after the train as it labored away. "Gawd sen' I ain' sold fur away fum Betty!" he muttered.

II

THE JOLIBOIS DANCING—ACADEMY.

MADAME ANATOLE DE JOLIBOIS and her maiden sister, Miss Serena Dibbs, were the joint owners of the odd-looking, many-porched, weather-beaten house into which little Olive Herring had disappeared under the abstracted gaze of John Thornham. Here they lived, alone, the only surviving members of a hard-working respectable family, whose head — a master-carpenter with ideas — had built the house with his own hands in the palmy presidential days of Thornham. It rambled about the large space allotted to it in a fashion of its, or rather of Mr. Dibbs's own, bulging here and there into unexpected and wholly irrelevant bows, and swells, and octagons, and bristling at every angle with little windowless turrets which served no apparent purpose. The hall which divided it in half was — relatively — baronial in size, and had been a sore vexation to the late Mrs. Dibbs by reason of the bare floors and the daily waxing and polishing thereof then in vogue.

This housewifely duty, however, after their mother's death, had been less vigorously exacted of themselves by the doubly orphaned Dibbs sisters — until the inception of the Dancing-Academy.

Madame Anatole de Jolibois, or Miss Kizzy, as she was familiarly and affectionately called by the townspeople, — a tall, angular, heavy-jawed woman, with curiously deep-set, dark soft eyes and a bossy nose, — was the elder of the two sisters. As Miss Dibbs some years earlier, she had possessed, beside a half-interest in the Dibbs homestead, a tidy sum in bank. To this she added from time to time continued savings from her slender salary as assistant music-teacher at the Thornham Female Seminary, where her younger sister was in process of being " finished."

Miss Keziah, despite her angularity, her plebeian birth, her nose, and her deplorable want of taste in matters of dress, had attracted the attention of Monsieur Anatole de Jolibois, Professor of Music and The French Language at the Seminary; and after a brief but ardent courtship, this ele-

gant and dapper person, some years her
junior, had actually led her to the altar — as
she herself expressed it. Thornham held up
its hands in amazement over this extraordinary proceeding; but it fell into spasms
of retrospective prophecy when, in less than
a week after the wedding ceremony, Monsieur de Jolibois disappeared without the
formality of a leave-taking, carrying with
him the whole of Miss Kizzy's hard-earned
and carefully hoarded money, withdrawn
from the bank by herself the day before, and
affectionately confided to the better judgment of her newly made spouse.

The faculty of Thornham Female Seminary, which with flattering haste had ele-
vated Madame de Jolibois to a "full profes-
sorship" in the college, dismissed with equal
promptitude the abandoned bride from all
connection with that institution, as a person
unfit longer to initiate its high-bred pupils
into the mysteries of the scales.

For a short time thereafter, her gaunt
figure was seen passing about the winding
walks of her garden; or lingering on one
of Mr. Dibbs's Grecian porticoes, as if ex-
pectant of her lord's return. The few old
friends who ventured to offer sympathy

were received with a quiet dignity, and a grace quite new to a Dibbs; but born, presumably, of an overwhelming sense of her disgrace.

One morning, quite as suddenly as the graceless Frenchman himself had vanished, Madame de Jolibois also disappeared. Miss Serena, even then showing symptoms of the extraordinary obesity which in later years won for her the sobriquet of Miss "Fatty" Dibbs, remained alone in the house, red-eyed and forlorn, but reticent. This, too, was most unusual for a Dibbs! It excited comment. In fact, the Dibbs family, small as it was, occupied, during the whole of that lazy monotonous summer, more of the attention of Thornham than it had done since Jed Dibbs, alone and unaided, had planned and reared his turreted mansion.

"Spiteful old thing!" cried the fluttering Seminary girls, when they learned of Miss Kizzy's departure. "She is *pursuing* that dear, handsome, *unhappy* Monsieur Anatole!"

"Jollyboys is catching it, shore," chuckled the gossips under the Man-Fig; "an' serves him right, durn him. Why 'n't he stay in Asia — or whatever island he come from."

"Poor Miss Kizzy!" sighed the older women. "She has no doubt crept off somewhere to hide her broken heart. And *whatever* will Serena Dibbs do, for a living!"

Exactly six months later, Madame de Jolibois returned; and a circular, written in her own fine slanting hand, was carried by Liberty, Miss Elinor Thornham's colored butler, from house to house throughout Thornham.

It announced that Madame Anatole de Jolibois, having studied the Saltatory Art at the Celebrated Institution of Madame Zémire Soladelle, in New Orleans, would on the 15th of October open in the Hall of her Residence a Dancing-School for Children of Both Sexes.

Especial attention paid to Deportment.

Hours from 3 to 4 on Tuesdays and Thursdays, 9 to 11 on Saturdays.

Under the Patronage of Miss Elinor Thornham.

N. B. Music Supplied by Miss Serena Dibbs.

The last clause explained — and justified — Miss Serena's continued and vigorous thumping of the *Lancers,* the *Evergreen Waltz,* and the *Lydia Schottische* on the tinkling old piano during the lonely months of her sister's absence.

Just why Miss Kizzy had chosen this particular profession, no one but herself ever knew. But she carried into it the conscientious painstaking and scrupulous integrity of purpose which characterized all her actions; and though, as June Badgett allowed, it was a "plum sight" to see her with lifted skirts and out-turned elbows, setting her large gaitered feet into the correct First Five Positions for the edification of her pupils, or leading them through the mazes of a Virginia reel, yet her patrons had just cause for self-congratulation. The little girls, at least, flocked eagerly to their lessons; and some contended that an improvement in the deportment of the very young gentlemen of Thornham was plainly perceptible.

Furthermore, it presently became apparent that the reserve of Madame de Jolibois was not, as had been conjectured, the result of an acute sense of her position as a deserted wife, but pride in the importance of her married estate.

"You must understand Serena," she said impressively, "that a married woman, and especially the wife of a *dee* Jollyboys, should consider her honorific position, and conduct herself accordingly. Monshur dee Jollyboys indeed may return at any moment, from — from his important Mission Abroad."

And Miss Serena, who believed implicitly whatever Miss Kizzy believed, held up her head proudly, and spoke with calm confidence of Brother Anatole's return.

The Jolibois Dancing-Academy had now flourished for nearly ten years, and, although Monsieur de Jolibois gave no sign of repentance or return, before she died, Miss Thornham had the satisfaction of knowing that her old friend and protégée had opened another bank account, and was in a fair way to be under shelter should a rainy day overtake her.

.   .   .   .

Miss Serena's heart gave a thump, for, peering through a crack in the door, she caught sight of a strange man. He had unfastened the front gate and was standing, hat in hand, gazing at a little figure which was running toward the house between the double row of red hollyhocks and larkspur. "Brother Anatole has returned," she murmured, untying her apron hurriedly, and thrusting her shuck-mop into a corner. But another peep showed her the clear strong profile of John Thornham as he turned and walked away in the direction of Newall's office.

"No," said Miss Kizzy at her elbow. Her voice was slightly tremulous. "No, I am not expecting Monshur *dee* Jollyboys *to-day*. Still, Serena, you should be careful to lock the front doors when we are waxing and polishing. It would certainly vex Monshur Anatole if he should discover his wife and sister engaged in so menial an occupation. 'Why, Olive Herring!'" she added, looking down at the child who had slipped noiselessly in, "you are full ten minutes early. Run into the yard, child, and wait for the others."

Olive obeyed. The sisters — their skirts pinned above their knees, and their sleeves carefully protected by brown-paper bags — resumed their interrupted labor, pushing the mops up and down the dark floor, which already shone like a mirror, reflecting the lank spare figure of the one, and the quivering shapeless mass of the other.

A sudden rush of feet without, and a shrill chorus of angry young voices, disturbed the steady swish-swash of their

brooms.   They disappeared, after a glance
at the clock, into the privacy of their own
apartment, whence half a minute later
Madame de Jolibois emerged, her black silk
skirts shaken down, her sleeves released
from the paper bags, and a red rose (in
memory of the one which Monsieur Anatole
had gallantly fastened there on the day of
their betrothal) adorning her scant gray
locks.

She opened the front door. Her Saturday morning pupils — twenty or more in
number — had swarmed up the steps and
were clustered on the porch, buzzing like so
many angry hornets.   In their midst, and
apparently the head and front of the unwonted disturbance, stood Olive Herring.
Her arms were thrown protectingly about
a bare-headed sobbing girl of her own age.
Her head was lifted defiantly, her lips were
compressed, her dark eyes flashing; she
looked comically like a small Fury. But
Miss Kizzy saw no humor in the situation.

"What is the matter, children?" she
demanded sternly.

For one moment the belligerents were
overawed. Then a clamor of cries and
ejaculations filled the air.

“ Please ’m, it was Rose Drennon’s fault.”

“ Jed Bates he jerked Rose’s hair-ribbin.”

“ Kitty Wash’n’ton she up ’n’ said ” —

“ Olive Herring ” —

“ Dunc Jeffrey he whacked Jed on the head ” —

“ ’T wa’n’t me, Miss Kizzy ” —

“ I did n’ say nothin’ ” —

“ Jed he jerked Rose’s hair-ribbin, ’n’ Olive she ” —

“ What is it all about, Duncan ? ” interrupted the dancing-mistress, turning to one of the older boys, — a freckle-faced, blue-eyed, frank-looking lad of fourteen, who stood somewhat apart, endeavoring to hide the purple scratch on his cheek with his straw hat, and furtively brushing the dust from his jacket.

“ I’d — I’d rather not tell, please ’m, Miss Kizzy,” he stammered, flushing scarlet.

“ Hit’s thess this-a-way, Miss Kizzy,” piped one of the smaller boys, eager for distinction. “ We uz all out in th’ yard, by th’ honeysuckle arbor, waitin’ fer Miss Fatty — I mean Miss S’rena, please ’m — to open the do’; ’n’ Rose Drennon she had on a new hair-ribbin, ’n’ Jed Bates he come up behine her ’n’ jerked her hair-ribbin, ’n’ she thess slapped Jed in the face, 'n' Kitty Wash'n'ton she said Rose wa'n't nothin' but po' white trash, no how, 'n' all the girls laughed, 'cep'n' Olive Herring, 'n' Rose begun to cry, 'n' Dunc he whacked Jed; 'n' Jed 'n' Joe Hopson jumped Dunc, 'n' scratched his face 'n' tore his jacket, 'n' Van Herring helped Dunc, 'n' we heard the clock a-strikin', 'n' we all run, 'n' Olive she put her arms roun' Rose 'n' sassed ever'body, 'cep'n' Dunc; 'n' ever'body sassed Olive back, 'cep'n' *me* 'n' Dunc 'n' Van, 'n' '' —

"This is scandalous!" cried Madame de Jolibois, throwing her hands up despairingly. "Ten years, Serena," she continued, with impressive slowness, " have I taught grace and politeness to the young ladies, and deportment to the young gentlemen of Thornham, and never before has a ribald altercation — a contest — a combat — a — a fight, I may say, taken place within these precincts. If Monshur *dee* Jollyboys had witnessed it, he would have been justly shocked. I tremble lest he should return at this moment!"

She drove her flock before her into the wide hall, and locked the door behind her. There, standing the delinquents in a row along the polished floor, she administered a many-syllabled and scathing rebuke, which many of them — now middle-aged men and women — remember with awe to this day.

A shamefaced apology was tendered by the whole school — who repeated it after Miss Kizzy, like the General Confession — to the pretty blonde little girl whose brilliant green hair-ribbon had been the primary cause of the disturbance; and the scratched and battered combatants reluctantly shook hands.

"I think Duncan Jeffrey is as *brave* as a *lion*," Olive Herring whispered audibly, though to nobody in particular, as that young gentleman backed away after this disagreeable ordeal. Her eyes were fixed demurely on the toes of her dancing-slippers; but the boy caught a shy sidelong glance from beneath the long lashes. And at that precise moment, the feeling was born within him which was to grow with his growth and strengthen with his strength, even unto his life's end!

Rose Drennon, the motherless child of a sluggish, uncouth laborer, who "jobbed" about the gardens and door-yards of Thornham, dried her eyes, bridling in conscious

triumph ; and, forgetting her crumpled hair-
ribbon, stood up with one of her late tor-
mentors for the Lancers.

Miss Serena settled herself upon the
piano-stool, which creaked under her weight,
and spread her pudgy hand over the yellow
keys.

Miss Kizzy unlocked the door, and threw
it open to the honeysuckle-laden air that
came floating in. "*Now*, if Monshur dee
Jollyboys should chance to arrive — by way
of the river, Serena — for as I have fre-
quently observed to you, Monshur Anatole
prefers to travel by water — he will find us
ready to receive him in a becoming manner.
Courtesy to your partners ! Swing corners !
Simms Reeves, take your fingers out of your
mouth !   Hold up your shoulders, Olive.
Balance all ! Not so fast, Serena. *Forward first four !   One, two, three !*"

And the Jolibois Dancing-Academy fell
suddenly into its accustomed routine.

III.

THE HERRING RIFLES.

ONE morning, some three weeks later, June Badgett halted his wagon and. team near the Man-Fig. He was too hurried to join his cronies there, having, he explained, contracted with Mis' Alsbury, the doctor's wife, to fetch her a wagon-load of preserving-peaches from the other side of the river. But he plainly had something on his mind, — something unpleasant, judging from the expression on his red face. The suggestion of a frown appeared between his small nondescript - colored eyes. He dropped the reins over one foot and extracted a plug of tobacco and a buck-knife from his trousers-pocket. "Johnny Thornham is biggaty to the plum last," he finally remarked, stuffing a generous cut of "Nigger-head" into his mouth.

"Johnny Thornham!" echoed Drennon, who had slouched forward and stood with an elbow on a front wheel. "He ain't here!"

"I know he ain't," retorted June, "an'

that's the p'ison meanness of it, durn him!"

"What has he done?" demanded Tuke Chancellor curiously.

"Done? Well, sir! What do you s'p'ose is goin' on out yander at Miss Elinor Thornham's at this durned hot minit? A *private sale*, sir. Common folks ain't er-lowed to buy Johnny Thornham's mules an' niggers, much less 'n his ole chairs an' tables an' sofys!"

"Who says so?" called Jimmy Hopson from his perch on the broken fence.

"*I* say so, sir! I saw Pete Newall settin' on a bench in Miss Elinor's rose-garden jes' now; an' a passel o' men, the Lord knows who, roun' the back gall'ry, an' I hitched an' started to go in. Ding ef Pete Newall did n't have the gall to tell me that it was a private sale. 'By Mr. John Thornham's orders, Mr. Badgett,' he says mighty slick, takin' off his hat. Ole Josh Cameron was sellin' of the niggers off'n the back steps. I heerd him a-hollerin' ez I drove away. Johnny Thornham's orders — an' he a thou-san' miles off yander in New *Orleens!*"

"I saw Van Herrin' go in there awhile ago as I drove by," remarked Welsh.

"I thought he had gone off somewhere out'n reach o' jedgment," Jimmy said, idly swinging his legs and knocking his heels against the fence.

"He come back yistiddy on the train. I seen him over at the *dee*-po'. He ain't afeard o' no jedgment. He knows no Thornham ain't goin' to have the law on no other Thornham!" and Drennon laughed triumphantly up in Badgett's face, his dull eyes gleaming for a second with something like satisfaction.

"There 's somp'n worse 'n the jedgment o' the courts, or o' Johnny Thornham either," said Badgett sententiously, "an' that 's the jedgment o' God. You wait tell you see it strike Van Herrin'. Not that I 've got anything ag'in' Van," he went on in a reflective tone, "but I wish my Maker may strike me stone dead ef I did n't see him with my own eyes come out'n Miss Elinor's settin'-room the night she died, an' was robbed."

"He ain't never said he wa'n't there, ez I know of," declared Drennon.

"God-a-mighty! I 'd like to see the man that 'ud dare to *ast* him ef he was there," cried Badgett.

He gathered up the reins and clucked to his mules.

"What's your hurry, June?" demanded Welsh lazily.

"Hurry! Mis' Alsbury has had her brass kittles on the fire ever sence sun-up a-waitin'. Gimme the tobacco, Rufe. I ain't got time to spit, much less 'n to set here an' wait tell you saw off a chaw with that ole Barlow-knife o' yourn."

Nevertheless he did not go. He looked anxiously over his shoulder from time to time, making a feint of examining the split-baskets piled in the deep wagon-body. The sleek mules moved their long ears back and forth and whisked their stumpy tails, aware that the clucking was only a pretense unless accompanied by a flick of the rawhide whip. Drennon slouched back to his place against the Man-Fig. The conclave remained expectantly silent.

"*Private sale,*" repeated Badgett to himself wrathfully. "D—n Johnny Thornham! Ez ef his mules an' niggers, an' ole crock'ry-ware, was too good fer common folks to look at, much less 'n buy."

A black object appeared in the middle of the road toward Roseneath. It advanced slowly under the broiling sun, raising such a cloud of dust that even Jimmy Hopson's keen eyes failed for some time to recognize the man approaching them. He stood upon the fence shading his eyes with his hand.

"It's Lib Thornham," he announced at length, "and Miss Elinor's old dog, Magnus, gallopin' 'roun' in the dust. Hello, Lib," he continued, as the negro drew near. "Have you been on the block?"

"Yes, sah," replied Liberty, touching but not removing his hat.

"You did n't fetch much, I reckin," Jimmy went on facetiously; "not more 'n a couple o' hundred."

"I fetched nine hundred dollars, cash," returned Liberty, with dignity. "I ain' carpenter, an' bricklayer, an' butler fer nothin'." His tone, though not insolent, had that undercurrent of familiarity which betrays the invariable contempt of the negro for the "poor-white."

"Who bought you, Lib?" asked Chancellor.

"Mr. Vanborough Herring," replied Liberty, his thick lips parting in a pleased laugh which showed his strong white teeth.

"God-a-mighty!" ejaculated Badgett,

dropping his lines in his amazement, and standing up in his seat.

The negro touched his hat again and walked on, the Newfoundland, with red lolling tongue and slobbering jaws, trotting after him.

There was a moment of profound silence.

"Well," said June at last, with an air of conviction, "well, gentle*men*, that settles it! Nine hundred dollars! Van Herrin', to my certain knowledge, ain't had a law-case fer more 'n twelve months, ner a pair of new boots fer six. Nine hundred dollars cash fer Lib Thornham, an' the Lord knows what else he ain't bought out yander at Johnny Thornham's private sale. That settles it, don't it? He's been off som'ers an' sold one of them di'mons he stole from Miss Elinor, that 's what he 's done."

.   .   .   .

When Liberty reached the pretty vine-clad cottage where the Vanborough Herrings lived, he paused in an angle of one of the squat outside brick chimneys and gave a low whistle. This brought his wife, Betty, — a comely young negress with sleek black cheeks, a flat nose, and wide smiling mouth, — to the kitchen door. She looked about, frowningly, turning a plate in her shapely hands.

"Is dat you, Lib?" she called in a cautious tone. "Lawd, I wonder does dat triflin' nigger think I ain' got nothin' to do cep'n' to stan' in dis do' an' lis'n fer dat whissle o' his'n!"

She raised her voice, bridling coquettishly. Then, as Liberty did not appear, an anxious look came into her great yellow-brown eyes. "Hit's a bad sign," she muttered uneasily, "a mon'sus bad sign to hear a pusson's whissle, an' dat pusson ain' in de presence. Oh Gawd! what's dat?" She threw her apron over her head and sank trembling into a chair, as Magnus, behind the chimney with Lib, uttered a low whine. "I know'd it!" she moaned; "fus a whissle, an' den a dog-howl, an' nobody in de presence. Somp'n turrible is comin' to me! Lib 's been put on de block an' sold out'n de county! Oh Lib, Lib!"

"Name o' Gawd, Betty, what's de matter?" cried Liberty, springing into the kitchen and dropping on the floor at her feet.

Betty uncovered her head to look at him. Her face on a level with his, as he knelt before her, was working painfully.

"Lib," she whispered, "has you been put on de block?"

Liberty nodded.

"Den who — who is yo' new marster?"

"*Mars Van Herrin'*," shouted Lib, jumping to his feet and lifting her in his powerful arms. "Me an' de dog has come home, Betty! *Home*, gal! Fer de res' of ou' lives, me an' Miss Elinor's ole dog! De *patter-roller* ain' gwine ter have a chance ter ketch me no mo'! I gwine ter cut wood an' fetch water fer de laklies black woman in Texas!"

"Git along, you fool nigger," cried Betty. And their joyous laughter rang in chorus upon the still air.

.   .   .   .

All Thornham shared the wonder and excitement of the Man-Fig council over Vanborough Herring's unwonted journey, — whose object and destination remained a mystery, — and his purchase of the valuable negro, Liberty. The excitement increased almost to frenzy six months later when it transpired that he had become the owner of Roseneath itself, which had been thrown back by a dissatisfied buyer into Newall's hands.

June Badgett had struck the note; he had coined the phrase, "*He has sold Miss Thornham's diamonds.*" There were those who uttered this charge openly and with confidence. Others affected not to believe it, yet secretly accepted it as a possible solution of the sudden change in Vanborough Herring's fortunes. Others, again, laughed the whole story to scorn, affirming that the necklace itself was a myth, no one in Thornham ever having seen the mistress of Roseneath wear such an ornament. A few were stoutly indignant. Among these last were Peter Newall and Madame Anatole de Jolibois.

"He is incapable of such a cowardly crime," mused the lawyer to himself, laying down his pen in the midst of a letter to John Thornham, wherein he mentioned that Roseneath had been resold, but refrained from naming its latest purchaser; "yet he was with her that night — God forgive me for never having told of it, if he is guilty! I saw him enter the door which she herself opened for him. . . . He could not have done anything so base. . . . Where can he have obtained money for the purchase of Roseneath! . . . If he would only speak.

. . . If he would only be less reticent with me. . . . But, then, he has never forgiven me for loving her too."

"It is a monstrous lie, Serena," remarked Miss Kizzy, with her mouth full of pins — for it was waxing and polishing day at the Dancing-Academy. "A monstrous and inconceivable prevarication. Something must be done about it. I will consult Monshur *dee* Jollyboys when he returns from his Foreign Mission. Get out the mops, child. And be sure and give the Herring children some of that fruit-cake when they come."

Amid this buzz of village gossip, the Vanborough Herrings took possession of their new home. Herring himself superintended the replacing and arranging of the old Thornham furniture, — much of which he had acquired at the sale, — showing an almost feverish wish that each familiar object should stand in its accustomed place. His pretty young wife, delicate-looking, but hitherto gay and light-hearted, moved somewhat thoughtfully about the stately many-roomed mansion. Olive slipped into it as if it had been her own by birthright. The boy, Young Van, two years older, seemed, like his mother, from the very first to fall under some subtle spell beneath the new roof-tree: his dark thin face became strangely melancholy; his eyes at times followed his father about with a questioning look which made an uneasy silence among older people, and hushed even the noisy glee of little Jack and little Jeanie, the two younger children.

It was gay enough in other respects— Roseneath! Its lavish hospitality kept pace with Vanborough Herring's success. For success— the success in his profession for which he had striven so long, so arduously, and so abortively— had come to him with that first mysterious turn in his fortunes. It was suddenly discovered that he had a profound knowledge of the law. His good luck, as his fellow townsmen called it, became proverbial. Even those who had most industriously circulated the story of the stolen jewels, hastened to employ him when business of their own required a steady hand, deep learning, and quiet tact. His reputation extended, and his practice grew far beyond the narrow limits of his own county; and when, some years after he became the owner of Roseneath, he ran for the Legislature of his State, he was elected by an overwhelming majority. In the midst of

his almost phenomenal career, the wealthy
and influential legislator retained the unapproachable, half - repellent attitude, which
had imperceptibly superseded the open,
frank, and joyous manner of the struggling
young lawyer.

"It's his conscience that makes him so
hide-bound, that's what it is!" asserted
June Badgett.

"It's his dollars, that's ,what it is!"
grinned Tuke Chancellor in reply.

.   .   .   .

"I wonder how much of that abominable
gossip he has ever heard," thought Newall,
one evening as he sat at dinner at Roseneath.
Herring's clear-cut stern face was turned
toward the pretty woman on his right.   She
was relating, with great vivacity and many
embellishments, the story of the Man-Fig to
the guest of honor, — a distinguished judge
from the capital.

"The blood of the murdered Don Manuel
Gayoso y Gonzalvo used to *ooze* from the
big purple figs," she was saying, and an affected shiver shook her bare white shoulders,
— "and they say his ghost continues to haunt
the spot.   If it does," she continued gayly,
"it has company enough!   For the ghosts

of murdered reputations must be pretty thick there! And if any there be among us who has lied or stolen, let him beware of the Man-Fig Council."

At this unexpected and malapropos climax, an uncomfortable thrill passed around the table. The narrator flushed, biting her lips, and dropped her eyes upon her plate, presumably praying the earth to open and swallow her. The distinguished guest, alone, unaware of the inadvertent allusion, calmly continued to eat his dinner. Newall thought that Mrs. Herring's pale face changed its expression. He glanced furtively at his host. Herring's impassive face reassured him. "She knows, perhaps," he sighed inwardly. "Poor little lady! But I am sure he has never heard it. Thank God. For even in heaven where she is, Elinor Thornham would not be happy if he were suffering."

His head sunk between his shoulders, and, oblivious of the renewed hum of conversation around him, his thoughts wandered back into a past which included none but himself and a

"Dear dead woman, yet unpossessed."

Newall had aged unaccountably during

the past few years; his hair was sprinkled with gray; the wrinkles about his eyes had deepened; his broad shoulders drooped. Herring on the contrary — full a year older — retained all the spring and elasticity of youth. His dark eyes were filled with fire; his lithe erect figure was instinct with life and vigor. But for the rigid lines about his mouth, and the heavy furrow between his straight brows, he might have been that Van Herring of a dozen years back, who had wooed — in this very house — and jilted the beautiful and high-spirited Elinor Thornham.

. . . .

Newall came out of his reverie with a start. There was a clatter of horse's hoofs upon the shelled drive outside; a spurred heel rang on the gallery, and a man, reeling with fatigue, came unceremoniously into the dining-room, with an envelope in his hand.

It was a messenger bringing to Vanborough Herring the news of the surrender of Fort Sumter.

. . . .

Within the month, the Herring Rifles, uniformed and equipped at the expense of their captain, — Herring himself, — were mustered into the Confederate States Service. Jimmy Hopson, with a long knife in his belt, and a look of grim defiance on his round boyish face, was among them; and Tuke Chancellor, mildly interested in "tic-tacs"; and young Duncan Jeffrey, his yellow curls and beardless cheeks in strange contrast with the rugged visage and grizzled locks of his great-uncle, Major Billy Duncan, a veteran of the Texan War for Independence, and of the Mexican War with the United States.

They went away one balmy May morning. The entire population of Thornham — men, women, and children — thronged about the station, shouting themselves hoarse, throwing up hats and caps, and waving tear-wet handkerchiefs, as the train drew slowly up the road. The "boys" in their brand-new uniforms crowded the platforms, looking back, laughing and singing, all filled with a mad haste to know somewhat of that fair game, in which they were to play a losing part. The sleek black faces of their body-servants grinned from the car windows.

Liberty had climbed to the top of the rear coach and stood there, his huge form outlined against the sky.

"Good-by, Betty-gal," he shouted. "Tek

keer o' de pickaninnies an' Miss Elinor's
dog! Good-by, Miss Jeanie. Good-by,
little Miss Olive! I 'm gwine ter tek keer
o' little Mars Dunc an' de Cap'n ! ''

"Will you lend Liberty to me until the
war is over?" Herring had asked playfully
one day, looking down, with one of his rare
smiles, into his little daughter's face.

"Yes, papa," she had gravely returned.
She had "claimed" Lib, as young Van had
appropriated Magnus, from the moment
they appeared at the cottage. "He will
take care of you."

Duncan Jeffrey was standing near his
captain, who was completing the preparations for departure. The tall youth of
eighteen looked bashfully at the eleven-year-
old child.

"And of me, Ollie," he said, blushing, he
could not have told why; "may Lib take
care of me too?"

.   .   .   .

And so the Herring Rifles went up to
"the front," — that vague border-land between friend and foe, kinsman and kinsman,
brother and brother, — ignorant, gay, defiant, hopeful. God in Heaven help you, lads,
— and the lads across the border!

"For a soldier is a gentleman, his honor is his life,
  And he that won't fight at his post shall ne'er stay with
    his wife,
    Shall ne'er stay with his wife.
  And he that won't fight at his post shall ne'er stay with
    his wife." [1]

"Farewell, sweethearts, 't is for awhile, oh dear sweet
    girls, adieu,
  And when the war is over, we 'll come and stay with you !
  Yes, when the war is over, boys, we 'll then sit down at
    ease,
  And plough and mind, and press and grind, and do
    just as we please,
    Just as we please,
    Just a-s w-e p-l-e-a-s-e ! "

The refrain came echoing back from the rich and tangled bottom-lands into which the train had plunged, and the answering cheer that followed after was faint and feeble, for it struggled through aching throats.

June Badgett and Rufe Drennon returned to the Man-Fig whose straggling shade was grateful in the noonday heat. There Dudley Welsh presently joined them. He had a shamefaced look, and his eyes were red. " Dinged if I ain't goin' too," he declared, dropping into his accustomed place at the foot of the tree.

" I ain't," said June cheerfully. " I ain't

----

[1] A Confederate camp-song.

got time to spit, much less 'n to go to the war. Let Van Herrin' do the fightin', — him an' them yether fellers up yander at Austin that drug Texas out'n the Union. He's mighty free of his money, Van is; a-fittin' out the Herrin' Rifles! An' the las' thing, the plum las'! he done before he lef' was to up an' buy Fair View Plantation an' stock it with niggers, an' mules, an' a overseer; an' set it a-goin'. He's powerful free of his money. But I ain't fergot how he got it. Jes you wait ontel the jedgment o' God falls on him. I ain't got nothin' ag'in' Van, but I wish my Mak— Hello, there 's Mis' Herrin' an' the childern!"

"She's got my Rosy in there," said Drennon, shuffling to his feet and staring after the carriage. There was a note of exultation in his monotonous voice.

Mrs. Herring leaned back, pale and exhausted, among the cushions. The little girls on the front seat — Olive, and Rose Drennon — were chattering gayly and singing snatches of the soldiers' farewell ditty. But Young Van, the slim, sad-eyed boy, pressed against his mother, flushing painfully, and turning his head as they rolled past the Man-Fig.

Betty had preceded them home, and Madame de Jolibois awaited them on the front steps.

"Don't you fret yo'se'f, Miss Jeanie, honey," Betty exhorted, helping her mistress to alight, and gathering little Jack and little Jeanie in her arms. "D' ain' nothin' gwine to happen to Mars Van. Gawd sen' dat nigger Lib don' git his-se'f killed, foolin' roun' dem Yankees," she added, under her breath.

"I know what it is, dear Mrs. Herring," said Miss Kizzy tenderly. "I am aware of the poignancy of your feelings. I have also an absent husband and spouse. But they will return. Monshur dee Jollyboys and Vanborough will return loaded with honors. They may pass through the Tempest of Battle where the loud thunders rattle, but they will return. Together perhaps, for I am firmly convinced that Monshur Anatole has flown on the wings of patriotism to the aid of his adopted country. And — and, my dear, I will come once or twice a week to Roseneath to instruct Olive and Young Van in their steps. But — I have been unable to consult Monshur dee Jollyboys, who has been absent on a delicate and dangerous Mission — but Serena and I have decided to close the Jollyboys Dancing-Academy until the war is over. We do not deem it proper that we should continue to teach the Saltatory Art while our country is in the midst of bloodshed and tribulation."

IV.

EVERYBODY knows how it all ended!
The Herring Rifles came limping home, by
twos and threes, — ragged, forlorn, footsore,
hungry, — with defeat, stamped on their
wan faces. There were not many of them
left, to be sure! Jimmy Hopson, with a bullet through his brain, was sleeping yonder
on the bloody field of Gettysburg; Tuke
Chancellor had gone down — foremost in a
gallant charge — in the Battle of the Wilderness. You could have counted the dead
and missing by the number of black-robed
women who stole forth to gaze yearningly in
the faces of those who came, — asked a few
low-voiced questions, and fled weeping back
to their lonely chambers. Some among
those who returned were maimed for life.
Dudley Welsh had lost an arm; Uncle
Billy Duncan had a gash exactly across that
scar on his left cheek which he had fetched
home from Chapultepec; Colonel Herring,

promoted on the field for bravery, limped heavily from an unhealed wound in his knee; even June Badgett, who had, after all, found time to follow the Rifles with the first batch of recruits, was minus a couple of fingers.

"Hello, Rufe!" the latter exclaimed the day after his return, sauntering up to the Man-Fig in company with Welsh. "Have you been a-settin' here ever sence the war begun, durn yo' hide?"

Drennon got up from the patch of grass where he was lying. "No," he grinned, nowise abashed by the insinuation; "I was drafted inter the Home Gyard"—

"Home Gyard," interrupted June contemptuously. "I wish my Maker may strike me stone dead if He ever ketches me associatin' with a d——d white-livered skunk-eatin' Home Gyard!"

Nevertheless he remained, leaning his tired back against a post, for the fence was quite gone. He cast his eyes over the familiar scene. Nothing was changed,—in appearance at least,—a little more dilapidation here and there, perhaps,—a broken fence, a briar-grown front yard. But the same gray old stores, the glimpses of dark gables through the trees, the yellow sunlight warm on the one long street; the river, low and sullen between its bluffs; Jack Addington in the doorway of his warehouse (Thornham's only warehouse), shouting orders into space; the ferryman pulling at his rope ; the shaky train across the river, rounding the bend and rattling up to the station !   ("She" brought no thrill to June's breast now, however ; he had seen locomotives enough and to spare during his four years' service, had June !)   His gaze sought Roseneath in the midst of its great park-like lawn.

"Well," he mused rather to himself than to his companions, "some goes out privates an' comes back privates, an', lo, an' behole, their wagin-an'-team has been confiscated by a busted gover'mint, their wife an' chile is a-layin' out yander in the graveyard ; their do' is off'n its hinges an' jimpson-weed 's growin' in their co'n - patch !   Some goes out an' don't come back at all, an' their fam'lies mo'ns fer 'em.   But Van Herrin's luck shore sticks to *him !*   Stars on his coat-collar, Lib a-totin' his cyarpet-bag, *he* comes back to a standin' crop, nary mule gone fum his stables, a likely wife, an' a passel o' sassy childern ! "

It was true. Some mysterious charm seemed to brood over Herring's possessions. His very fences forbore to rot. The tremendous rise in the river which, one spring, had desolated the plantations above and below, had swirled around a bend somehow and left Fair View uninjured. His negroes, under a judicious and clear-headed overseer, had remained at work when neighboring fields were grass-grown for the lack of labor. Everything had thriven and increased, — live stock, cane, corn, grain, fruit. Even the rose-garden at Roseneath had never borne such a wealth of dewy, sweet-scented, velvet-leaved roses as in that dreary, despairing early summer of '65. His wife, whose boundless charities and sweet sympathy in a time of common suffering and common hope had endeared her anew to the community, had lost that look of anxiety and apprehension which had made her care-worn and prematurely old. She met her husband at the station, on his return, robust, joyous, radiant. Young Van, now a fine, manly lad, no longer shrank from companionship; Olive, blooming into exquisite girlhood; the two younger children glowing with health and spirits, — all this, as Badgett said, awaited the lucky man on his return.

One may, perhaps, be too fortunate.

Who was it unchained and set loose again that half-forgotten story? It would have been hard to say. A whisper, a look askance, a shrug of the shoulders, and the thing was done. Not even in the days which followed Vanborough Herring's first unaccountable gleam of prosperity did gossip rage more fiercely than now. Startling additions were made to the original text of the tale: Herring had wrested the necklet by force from the dying woman; there was a purple mark from brutal fingers on her throat when they found her! Some one during the war — somewhere — in New Orleans — in Chattanooga — in Richmond — had met the identical man to whom Herring had sold one, or a part, or the whole, of Elinor Thornham's diamonds.

"Wait till the Hand o' God strikes him!"

Once more June Badgett had coined the apposite phrase. It was in everybody's mouth, — *The Hand of God!*

"He was a gallant soldier," urged the unswerving minority.

"Of course!" retorted the majority contemptuously. "He hoped to make the world forget that he was a thief."

"He led many a gallant charge."

"Certainly; his conscience stung him so that he courted death."

"He bore every brunt with his men, and not the meanest ever appealed to him in vain."

"No doubt! A villain must ease his soul somehow."

.   .   .   .

"They do not scruple to accept his hospitality; they eat his food and drink his wine, and go their ways calling him a scoundrel and a thief!" said Newall bitterly, after a vain attempt to stem the tide of public opinion.

The cloud — for a time mercifully lifted — descended again upon the wife; her laughter died in her throat; she became silent and shrinking as before. Young Van gradually lost his youthful buoyancy.

If Herring, always reticent and self-contained, noted any of these things, or knew what they betokened, he made no sign.

Olive alone, on the threshold of womanhood, remained radiantly unconscious.

Meanwhile, Thornham slowly resumed its old-time uneventful routine. Save for the occasional presence of a uniformed officer representing the military government, and the groups of negroes loafing about the streets by way of realizing their freedom, there was little in the tranquil town to indicate that a world had tumbled about its ears.

Finally, and last of all, The Jolibois Dancing-Academy was reopened. A circular, written by Madame de Jolibois, and carried from house to house, as on a former occasion, by Liberty, urged its patrons to remember that the Growing Generation must be Educated, so that our Foes in future years may Respect them. Our Armies are Defeated, but there Remains with us the Consciousness of Right. Let us show the Enemy that we can Rise above Misfortune.

N. B. If any of my Patrons are unable to Pay, I will *gladly* Teach Their children without Compensation for the sake of the *Lost Cause.*

Miss Kizzy did not admit even to herself that her joints were a little stiff from misuse — and age. But she was secretly grateful when Olive Herring dropped in, as she sometimes did, and offered gayly to put the troublesome squad through its manual.

She leaned against the piano one March afternoon watching the young girl skim down the long hall with Duncan Jeffrey, who had come back from the war with a bullet in his shoulder, and a captain's stripe on his ragged gray sleeve. The children, aligned in two rows for a reel, gaped admiringly at their leaders.

Miss Kizzy's heart fluttered. She felt suddenly faint. "I am almost sure, Serena," she said in an undertone to her sister, "I have a presentiment that Monshur dee Jollyboys is about to return."

"Oh, yes," assented Miss "Fatty," playing stolidly on, "I am sure Brother Anatole is about to return."

"Do you know, Miss Kizzy," called Olive, rosy and breathless from swinging half-round and back with so many very young and bashful gentlemen, "do you know that there is going to be a ball at Roseneath next week? In honor of Van's nineteenth birthday. It happens to be my birthday, too. But I don't count. I am only seventeen," she added with a saucy glance at Duncan, who tried to say that she counted very much to one person at least, but stammered instead, and blushed, and held his tongue.

As for Miss Kizzy, Monshur Anatole for once went clean out of her head. Her face became stern. It was proper enough for the Growing Generation to learn its steps in order to insure respect of itself from the Enemy in future years. But for the actual generation to dance as it were on the ashes of the Lost Cause! That were sacrilege. But her eyes softened once more as the lithe young couple swayed forward again in the dance, the blonde head of the young ex-captain bent above Olive's brown curls, and her eyes smiling frankly into his.

A vision of Monsieur Anatole walking beside her in the Seminary grounds, that long-gone summer day, and plucking a rose for her hair, swam before her. "And, after all," she reflected, "it has been nearly two years since the surrender."

.   .   .   .

Even in the old days, when Steven Thornham — haughty and imperious, but magnificently open-handed in his mode of living — was master there, Roseneath never wore an aspect more royal than on the night of the ball given in honor of the oldest son of its present owner.   The countless glittering lights, the new and costly hangings, the gay garlands festooned from pillar to pillar of the large ballroom, the fairy-like nooks, bowered in palms, contrived here and there throughout the network of rooms and hall-ways, the smooth-swept lawn with its lantern-thridded trees — all this seemed little less than enchantment after the sombre, denuded years since the last ball in Thornham, — the ball at which the Herring Rifles in their trim new uniforms had danced the night before they marched away to " the front." Several of these scarred veterans looked on somewhat wistfully while more youthful feet beat the shining floors to the sound of joyous music.   Newall was one of these, for he too had worn the gray.   He sat unobserved in a corner of the sitting-room with its familiar furnishings, his eyes following the graceful motion of the dancers through a curtained doorway.

All Thornham was there.   Madame de Jolibois, sitting on a *causeuse* in a corner of the ballroom with Miss " Fatty " (both in wonderful toilettes created for the occa-sion), regretted aloud that Monshur dee Jollyboys could not have returned from his

Foreign Mission in time to be present. " Himself a brilliant luminary of the nobility of his native land, he would have beheld," she said, " the glittering aristocracy of this favored region." To her inmost self she breathed with a sigh of relief, "At last the slander is lived down! Thank God for Vanborough!"

Newall's gaze dwelt lingeringly upon Olive, whose dark luminous eyes filled him with vague remembrances. She stood beside her father at the upper end of the long ballroom. Herring's own eyes rested tenderly for a moment upon her joyous upturned face; then they swept over the assemblage. A flash of pride illuminated them, and a flush mounted to his dark cheek. He had indeed reason to be content. All Thornham was there! The struggling, ill-paid, well-nigh despairing lawyer of a decade back — to-day rich, prosperous, planter, legislator, judge — held his conquered world in the hollow of his hand! Newall, in his corner, felt an answering thrill. At that moment it seemed as if the sun blazing in the heaven of this man's life had at last dissipated every cloud and left the sky serene and smiling.

The lawyer heaved, like the dancing-mistress, a sigh of relief, and sank back into his seat. As he did so, a warm breath struck his cheek. He turned, startled. A face was pressed against the blind outside, and a pair of eyes peered eagerly into the room. Newall followed the direction of the absorbed gaze. Rose Drennon, pretty, blonde, blue-eyed, was among the dancers; Jed Bates's arm encircled her slight waist, her head drooped against his shoulder as they circled slowly down the crowded ball-room. The "poor-white" father was watching his child from the gallery! The lawyer shifted his position, affecting not to see the uninvited guest outside the window. It was then that a fragment of conversation reached him. A lady, full-blown and voluptuous-looking, with sleek black hair and narrow sensuous eyes, was sitting on Elinor Thornham's couch over against him. She was fanning herself coquettishly and chatting with a man who sat beside her, with his arm thrown along the back of the lounge. Their voices had probably been subdued hitherto, or Newall himself had been too absorbed to hear what they were saying. Now it seemed to him as if a thunder-tone assailed his ears.

"How many of the Thornham diamonds have gone into this, do you suppose?" the man asked with a meaning sneer on his long sallow face.

"Who can tell?" the woman responded, lifting her shoulders. "By. the way," she added, looking around her, "I believe that it was in this very room that he choked her and stole her diamonds. Do you think mine are safe from him?" And she made a pretense of shielding with her gloved hand the *rivière* of jewels adorning her own white throat.

A look of ineffable horror and anguish came into Newall's face. For Young Van, standing unnoticed in the embrasure of a window beyond the speakers, already pale and melancholy, grew absolutely livid. His lips parted; his limbs seemed to tremble beneath him; he made an uncertain step forward, then turned abruptly into the ball-room, glided silently through the dancers, and passed out upon the deserted veranda. "Poor boy! Poor lad!" sighed Newall aloud, for he was alone in the little room. The face behind the blind had disappeared, and the thoughtless gossipers had joined the tide which was beginning to flow toward the supper-room.

.   .   .   .

The gayety of the stately mansion had its grotesque counterpart out in the servants' quarters, where unctuous black valets and comely yellow maids aped the manners of their masters and mistresses, sitting in pompous and exaggerated decorum in Betty's cabin, or mincing in couples up and down the long kitchen-gallery. Crowds of humbler retainers from Fair View swarmed about the back yard, pressing up the steps and peeping through open windows ; and a score or more of pickaninnies, including Betty's five, patted *juba* and shuffled noisily under the trees to the sound of the fiddles in the " gret-house."

Liberty, whose gigantic frame seemed to have been enlarged and strengthened by the toil and hardship of camp-life, bustled with an air of importance between kitchen and supper-room ; now admonishing his own satellites in the pantry, now dictating to Betty and her corps of assistants about her oven-ringed fireplace.

" Be keerful o' dem cut-glass goblers, Jackson." "Pass in de *decanters*, Sam; don't you see dey is fair *dreened!*" "Come out'n dat do', Jess. Major Joe Burnham ain' tellin' dem jokes fer de likes o' you to laugh at!" "Betty, 'pears like you spec white folks kin wait tell mornin' fer dem oyshters. Hop eroun', gal, hop eroun'!"

"Git out'n my kitchen, Lib Thornham!" cried Betty, flustered. "I been over de fiah befo' ever I seed you. You ten' to yo' business ez de *butler* an' I'll ten' to mine ez de *cook! Gawd-a-mighty!*"

She dropped the spoon she was flourishing, and turned an ashen face on her husband. The old dog, Magnus, who had been lying in a corner of the fireplace, had dragged himself across the kitchen, and stood on the door-sill, howling mournfully, his purblind eyes strangely fixed, and his feeble body quivering.

"Dat ain' no hallelujah-whine like he sot up de day you an' him come into ou' fam'ly, Lib," Betty whimpered fearfully. "Dat's a *death-howl. O Gawd!*" — she shook from head to foot, clutching at his shoulder. For the steady long-drawn wail arose the third time on the air.

"Shet yo' fool mouth, Betty," said Liberty roughly. His own eyeballs were rolling and his teeth were hard upon chattering. "Ain't you see little Mars Van by de summer-house out yander in de rose-garden! De dog can't see out'n his *eyes*, but he's got innard sight. *He ain' altogether human, nohow, dat dog ain'*! He p'intedly knows dat his young Marster is settin' by his-se'f out yander in de rose-garden, in de moon-light."

.   .   .   .

The disordered house, the next morning, had that dreary, almost sinister air which follows a night of prolonged revelry. The sun streaming in at the wide-open windows shed a mocking light upon the wreckage of that high tide which had surged there a few hours agone, — fragments of lace, spangles, shreds of tulle and ribbon strewn upon the soiled and trampled floors; a fan tossed on a sofa, a pair of gloves forgotten on a mantel; here a filmy handkerchief breathing of its dainty owner, there a faded bouquet. Nothing so empty as a ballroom when the light feet of the dancers have left it!

The spurred heels of Young Van echoed jarringly on the silence as he crossed the ballroom to where his mother sat, alone and abstracted, on a divan with her hands folded idly on her lap. She looked up with a smile, but she avoided his searching gaze.

"I — I was just waiting for the servants to take it all down." She made a gesture toward the dying garlands that wreathed the walls.

"Mother," the boy said abruptly, "did you hear — were you — last night?" The words died away in a sob. He stooped and kissed her hastily, and strode away without looking back.

She followed him slowly, and stood watching from the gallery while he mounted the restive horse awaiting him, and galloped away for his morning ride. The slender young figure, erect and graceful in the saddle, disappeared in that turn of the road from which ten years before June Badgett had stood his fatal watch, and the mother went back into the deserted ballroom.

She had been a pretty woman, and a happy one in those old days when Vanborough Herring had not had a law-case for more than twelve months, nor a pair of new boots for six; but beauty and happiness had gone away together, suddenly — she could have named you the very day and hour!

They had come back for a brief space during the time that the women of Thornham
had wept and prayed together for their
absent husbands and sons and lovers, and
made lint and cartridges, with their hearts
beating in unison,—now with rejoicing, now
with dread,—and packed boxes for the
" boys " away yonder at " the front," with
mutual hopes and mutual fears.   Now, alas,
her thin face was again pinched and pitiful;
her large blue eyes were dim with much secret weeping.   Newall was right in his conjecture.   She did know! She had heard!
And, with a mother's intuition, she had long
ago divined that the boy, too, in some way,
had heard the shameful story which had
blasted his father's reputation in the midst
of worldly success.   But neither by word
nor look had mother or son betrayed to any
living soul — least of all to each other! —
their consciousness of the ever-blackening
cloud which hung above their lives; nor did
the wife know whether or not her husband
was aware of the foul stain upon his own fair
fame.   She had, indeed, seen a mask settle
and harden upon his face.   Did he, too, suffer?   Did he, too, writhe and groan in
secret?   She could not tell.   His tender-

ness toward herself was unabated ; his love and pride in his children were boundless. But an invisible barrier stretched there, where her soul would fain enter his and share with it all it might be fated to endure of pain or suffering, even of guilt and remorse.

She, too, had seen significant glances the night before, and caught the echo of half-uttered phrases.

She arose from the divan and began to walk aimlessly about the house, which she hated. Had its shadow not fallen across her own life and his ? And was it not here that the woman whom he had loved first —

She put the rising thought aside as unworthy of herself and him, and continued her lonely walk, avoiding instinctively the little nook which had been Elinor Thornham's sitting-room.

The voices of her children — little Jack and little Jeanie, romping on the gallery, and Olive in confidential talk with Liberty — at last penetrated to her troubled senses. She stopped to listen, glad of the relief.

The younger children scampered down the steps in hot pursuit of Betty's gang; and their boisterous shouts died away in the distance.

" Lawd, Miss Olive," Liberty was saying, " did n't I been an' tole you dat tale yis-*tiddy*! "

" I don't care, Lib," said Olive, " I want to hear it again."

They were in the butler's pantry. An occasional clatter of dishes mingled with their talk. Liberty was replacing the Thornham china in the tall presses built into the wall. Rose Drennon was with them.

" Shucks, chile," he returned. " Dat wa'n't a succumstanche! Mars Van was always doin' somep'n brash. He was de braves' man in ou' ridgment, Mars Van was! Lawd, I has seen him a-chargin' 'long, at de head o' de Rifles " —

" I know," interrupted Olive impatiently, " but that day the Rebel pickets were lying behind a low wall, when all at once the Federals came in sight at the edge of the woods, just beyond the old field. And a Rebel soldier jumped over the wall with a flag in his hand " —

" He wa'n't nothin' but a boy," interrupted Liberty in his turn, " a plum boy! An' his yaller hair a-flyin', an' his blue eyes a-shinin'! Lawd, Miss Olive, when dem bluecoats come in sight he jerked up de flag, an' whooped over dat wall like a streak o' lightnin', an' cut ercrost dat fiel' a-hol-lerin' an' a-wavin' de flag. All at once dey was a solingtary shot. It did seem like dem bluecoats did n' had de heart to shoot dat yaller-headed boy Reb! But de solingtary shot done struck him in de shoulder, an' down he come on his face on de groun' wi' de flag onder him. Den de bluecoats come a-chargin' todes him to git de flag. I tell you, Miss Olive, dey was like a swarm o' bees! De Rifle-boys jis lif' up dey heads an' drap 'em back, a-waitin'. But dreckly dey bus' out a-yellin' ontell you mought a' heard 'em down here in de Brazos bottom. Fer de cap'n, yo' pa, he riz up an' jumped dat wall like a stag-deer, an' whiz-z-z ercrost dat fiel'! And down he draps 'longside de boy. An' fus' thing we knowed, here he come *bookety-book!* wi' dat boy flung ercrost his shoulder, an' a-wavin' dat flag in his han'! An', Lawd, honey, by de time he gin me de boy to tek keer of dey *was* a scrimmage! An' we did n't git whipped — not *dat time*," he concluded with a chuckle of satisfaction.

"Ah," cried the girl, her clear voice ring-ing proudly, "my father is a hero! a hero, Liberty!"

"I ain' never tole you who dat fool yaller-headed boy was, has I, Miss Olive?" pursued Lib.

"Why no, who was it?"

"Well, hit was p'intedly little Mars Dunc Jeffrey, dat 's who."

"Was it?" said Olive, with less enthusiasm. "No wonder they made my father a Colonel for bravery," she added. "He ought to have been made a General."

"A hero!" echoed the wife, under her breath. Her tear-wet eyes were sparkling with pride. A girlish color had leaped into her worn cheeks. "A hero!" she repeated softly, smiling.

And then, what was it? A sudden and confused murmur of voices, a trampling of feet, a moan, as of some one or something in pain —

"Do not be alarmed, Mrs. Herring," Newall said, meeting her as she rushed forward with wildly beating heart, "Van"—

"My husband" — she gasped.

"No, Young Van. He has been thrown from his horse. We hope he is not seriously hurt. The doctor" —

She broke past him into the little morning-room whither they had carried the lad.

He was lying on Elinor Thornham's couch, moaning, but quite unconscious, with the blood oozing slowly from an ugly gash over his temple. The doctor was bending over him, busied already with bandages; his head rested upon his father's knee.

.   .   .   .

Toward nightfall, he seemed to recover consciousness. His eyes slowly unclosed, and, encountering his father's face, rested there for a moment with an expression of childlike love and confidence. Then a frown contracted his forehead. " Mother," he called out sharply, attempting to rise, " *Mother*, did you hear? . . . They said . . . diamonds . . . last night. My *father*. *My* father! " His voice rose to a shriek. " Long ago, when I was coming by the Man-Fig, mother, do you remember? They said he stole the diamonds. *Stole! My father!* "

A visible spasm of terror and dismay swept through the room. Liberty, standing at the foot of the couch, dropped the basin he held in his hands, and cowered to the floor. The men held their breath. Even the mother's agony for a second was in abeyance. She looked up at her husband with wide frightened eyes. His gaze was fixed

steadily upon the face on his knee; not a
muscle flinched, not an eyelash quivered
in his own. Miss Kizzy drew back into the
shadow of a curtain, overawed and trembling. Olive, with her head buried in her
mother's lap, did not look up; she alone had
not heard.

A long silence succeeded this scene. The
sun sank lower, and the level rays, streaming
in at the open window, fell full upon the
couch. A sudden puff of wind brought in a
scent of damask-roses from the rose-garden.
The boy smiled, — a rare smile that illuminated his pinched features. " Why, father !
. . . . Mother ! " he cried joyously, " we are
going back to the other house ! I am so
glad."

The eyes which had opened for an instant
closed; a fluttering sigh escaped from the
parted lips, — and Vanborough Herring continued to gaze on the dead face of his first-
born.

.   .   .   .

" It 's the jedgment o' God," said June
Badgett, in an awed tone, looking around
upon the Man-Fig Council. " The Hand o'
God struck him at las'."

" *The judgment of God !* " whispered

some even among those who followed the funeral cortége to the Thornham family burying-ground at Fair View. And so current was the expression that the Reverend James Hall, the old Rector of St. John's, deemed it needful, when he ascended the pulpit the following Sunday, to take as his text that stern admonition of our Lord, "*Judge not that ye be not judged.*"

.   .   .   .

Old Magnus, out in the kitchen, purblind, feeble, gaunt, knew, by that "inuard sight" which was his, when his little master in the great-house closed his eyes, to open them in that *other house* whither he went. And he also went his way, — following the lad, perhaps! who knows?

For, when Liberty and Betty came out of the little room, that night, where they were no longer needed, they found the dog in his accustomed place in the corner of the fireplace, dead, with his shaggy head between his paws.

V.

STORMED AT BY SHOT AND SHELL.

Young Van had been sleeping in the plantation cemetery at Fair View for half a year; it might indeed have been half a century, so rank and matted were the roses above his grave; so stained and mildewed the slender cross at its head!

.   .   .   .

Mrs. Hopson came out upon the back gallery at Roseneath. She had a shawl over her head, though the late August afternoon was warm and sultry; for Aunt Patty was getting on in years, and her blood had lost its heat. It was not the first time that the housekeeper had been left in charge of the place and its belongings. In the old days when Alcalde Steven Thornham made his exciting and often dangerous horseback trips about the sparsely settled country, or journeyed to Saltillo to confer with the Government of Coahuila and Texas, it was to Aunt Patty — then younger by many years, sturdy, clever, and masculine — that he confided the care of his wife and children, and the management of the house. During the prolonged absences of the family abroad and elsewhere, in later times, or of Elinor Thornham when Roseneath passed into her possession, it was still Aunt Patty who kept the shadowy rooms in order, and scolded and managed, and cared for the troop of idle house-servants.

After many years, she was once more temporary mistress there, Colonel Herring having taken his wife and the remaining children to a neighboring town, in the vain hope of finding some alleviation for the mother's silent and despairing grief over the death of her son.

"Hit's sholy a fine day, Miss Patty," called Betty from her cabin door, where she sat, fat and comfortable, with her brown and yellow brood tumbling about on the ground at her feet.

Mrs. Hopson traveled slowly down the steps with her hand on the rail, and walked across the kitchen - yard. Her eyes were fixed upon the western sky. The sun had set, but a band of coppery red stretched along the horizon, whence tongues of flame-tipped cloud shot up toward the zenith. A curious light filtered downward, suffusing the still air; the treetops swam in it, as in a sea of molten sulphur; the green of the grassplots and tufts of shrubbery beneath was changed to a sickly and livid yellow.

The old lady shook her head. " Don't talk to me about fine days, Betty, with that sky over us ! " she said impressively. " I 've seen that sky twice before in my lifetime, — once on the Gulf coast and once inland. Do you know what that sky means, Betty? *It means yellow fever !* "

" Lawd, Miss Patty, you don't sesso ! " cried Betty. " An' ou' white folks, an' Lib, yander, plum under de eedge o' dat yaller sky, I reckon ! Gawd-a-mighty sen' dat Miss Jeanie, ner Mars Van, ner Miss Olive, ner dem two chillen don' ketch it. Ez fer my ole man, I ain' nowise skeered 'bout him. Caze, you knows yo'se'f, Miss Patty, de yaller fever don't tetch niggers."

A month later the yellow fever broke out without warning on the Gulf coast; almost simultaneously it appeared in the town where the Herrings were staying; yet ten days, and it was declared epidemic; a rigid cordon of quarantine was drawn about the infected places, and an agonized cry went out for nurses.

The train that brought this news to Thornham carried on its outward trip the next day four passengers. The Reverend James Hall, tall, spare, and erect, in spite of his threescore and ten years, seated himself in the empty coach and deposited his traveling-bag beside him. He shook hands through the window with two or three of his parishioners who had come to see him off, and gazed a little wistfully over their heads — his lips moving as if in silent benediction — at the slim spire of St. John's rising above the treetops on the other side of the river. He frowned as Dud Welsh slouched awkwardly into the car and took a seat on the opposite side of the aisle.

"So you will not take my advice and stay at home, Dudley," he said. "You are running a great risk."

"So are you, sir," grinned the one-armed Dud, stretching out his long legs and thrusting his remaining hand into his trousers' pocket.

"I am doing my duty," said the Reverend Mr. Hall severely.

"So h I, sir," retorted Dud promptly, his bashful grin broadening.

At th moment there was a bustle among the slim crowd of idlers on the platform outside, and Aunt Patty Hopson and Madame de Jolibois were hoisted one after another up the steps, and ushered into the car. Miss Sona, her face swollen with weeping, handed in two well-worn carpet-bags, and turned away, sobbing aloud. Amid an ominous silence the train jerked forward and crept around the bend.

"I've had it," said Mrs. Hopson, cheerfully settling into her place, "and I ain't at all afraid."

"I ain't had it," Dud said, "but I've seen it. I'm not afeared, nuther. 'T ain't half as eery as goin' into a fight."

"I have not had it," observed the Reverend Mr. Hall in his slow soft voice, "and I have never seen it, but I am not afraid."

Miss Lizzy, looking out of the window, said nothing. She had not had it; she knew nothing about it; and afraid.

"And it, Ser toiled t ferry,

... if I did not go. ... ... boys ... the ribbon of ... ... in his buttonhole. I ... ... he here, he would command me to go.

They were on their way! — ... ... to the harvestriches town, into ... ... might enter, but where no ... within their guarded heart of ... would ... out. They had ... their... ... in ...... — ...: for already the living were hard ... to bury the dead, so swift and deadly ... the spread of the plague.

. . . .

When the late December frost ... came, the epidemic sensed for ... ... victims. The quarantine ... ... devastated town began ... ... breath and to count their ... ... long absent from Thornley ... home, — some of them!

Colonel Herring came, graver ... unapproachable than ever; Oliver, fragile ... ... life, and ...

them with a sort of hushed awe, as upon those who had come up from the bosom of the charnel-house.

Mrs. Herring, with little Jack and little Jeanie, was left behind in the wide grave which had received them all, the same day. Aunt Patty Hopson, her long service to the Thornhams ended, rested quite near. And the narrow ridge over against them covered the mortal remains of the Reverend James Hall, who went calmly about ministering to fever-stricken bodies and sin-sick souls, with the plague racking his own old frame, and passed over at length, even as Faithful did, holding by the hand one who, like Christian, was afraid.

VI.

A CONFESSION.

THE children went out decorously, one by one, turning at the door to make formal little bows "with the hand on the heart, and the hat gracefully lifted," or to drop solemn and antiquated "curcheys." Miss "Fatty" Dibbs waddled after them to see that the front gate was properly fastened. Madame de Jolibois sank red and panting on the horsehair sofa; drops of perspiration coursed their way along the wrinkles in her cheeks, and fell, dampening her muslin neck-erchief; the rose behind her ear drooped on its stem. Olive Herring, flitting about the dancing-hall, and humming under her breath the last tune which Miss Serena had drawn from the jangling piano, forbore to look at her. Miss Kizzy's profession, in truth, was beginning to be burdensome. Her joints were stiff; her step had grown heavy. But no one dreamed of suggesting her retirement. Thornham was, above all, conservative. It is quite likely that no one except Olive ever remembered to think that Miss Keziah was rising fifty, and might almost be regarded as an old woman; and quite likely, too, that Miss Keziah herself would have been aghast at the idea of intrusting the very young ladies and gentlemen of Thornham into other hands than her own.

"But she certainly will have to have an assistant," thought the young girl, glancing at her furtively.

"Olive," said Madame de Jolibois after a restful silence, "have you seen St. John's new preacher?"

St. John's, it will be remarked, was very low-church indeed. Nobody, as yet, had ever dreamed of calling its incumbent the Rector, or of addressing him as Father. Thornham referred to him as "the minister," "the preacher," or even "the parson," as if he were a mere dissenter. St. John's, indeed, differed from the other religious denominations in Thornham only in a sort of fictitious exclusiveness, which melted before the first Methodist quarterly meeting, or Baptist sociable.

The Reverend James Hall — wise, liberal, and saintly soul — had been the first and sole incumbent of St. John's. To the place left vacant by his death had been called the Reverend Mark Kennison, from one of the older States, — young, eager, and devout.

"No," returned Olive, interested, seating herself beside her old friend; "my father and I have been at Fair View ever since he came. Have you seen him, Miss Kizzy? Have you heard him preach? What is he like?"

Madame de Jolibois got up and went to the front door. "Serena!" she called to her sister, pottering about among the hollyhocks, "go around into the back yard and set Alexander H. Stephens on his feet. I heard him crow some time ago. Alexander H. Stephens, my dear," she explained over her shoulder, "is our new Cochin China rooster. Dr. Alsbury sent him to us last week. He is a most magnificent fowl. But, unfortunately, whenever he crows he topples over, and he cannot rise without assistance. Serena is obliged to set him on his feet several times a day. I am not *quite* sure that I did hear him crow this time," she added, coming back to her place on the sofa, "but Serena is very fond of him, and if she gets into the back yard where he is, she will re-

main until I remind her to return to the
house. The truth is, my child, I wanted to
get rid of Serena for a little while. I have
something on my mind," — her voice dropped
to a mysterious whisper. She grasped her
companion's shoulder and regarded her
searchingly. Olive clasped her hands.

"Oh, Miss Kizzy!" she breathed, trembling with delightful anticipation, "has Monsieur Anatole returned?" Monsieur Anatole, the radiant, romantic hero of her
childish dreams! She had never seen him,
— he had in fact departed on his "Foreign
Mission" before she was born, — but she
knew him well, that generous, high-minded,
brave, beautiful Frenchman, of whom Miss
Kizzy had talked to her ever since she could
remember.

"No, child, Monshur Anatole has not yet
returned, though I am expecting him at any
moment." She paused to rearrange the
faded rose in her hair. "I do not dare con-
fide in Serena. Serena is too excitable, and
she is sometimes indiscreet. She admitted
to Mrs. Washington the other day that
Tommy Doren has his lessons free. It is
true, Mrs. Washington wormed it out of
her! Well, young as you are, Olive, I

know I can trust you, and I cannot, I really cannot bear the dreadful burden longer alone."

"Oh, Miss Kizzy!" exclaimed Olive again, fairly beside herself with curiosity.

"It happened last fall," continued Madame de Jolibois solemnly, "the night after your poor dear mother was laid in her grave, with little Jack and little Jeanie; and before you yourself were taken down. Aunt Patty Hopson and I were nursing a family of poor people, — seven of them in the same room, and all with raging fever; two of the children past help, one already with black vomit. You know how it was, — the doctors exhausted, the nurses hardly able to stand on their feet from fatigue, the dead lying about waiting to be buried; the sick dying by scores, new cases reported every hour." Olive shuddered and grew pale, but the narrator, absorbed in her gruesome reminiscences, did not notice this. "It was after midnight when one of the doctors — a Dr. Robinson, a most interesting person — came to beg one of us to take charge of a man, — a stranger, who was down with the fever, and alone, in a house not far away. I went. The patient was a young man; he was delirious, and had, it appeared, but a slim chance for recovery. The doctor gave me some directions and went on his round, leaving me in sole charge of the patient. Toward morning, he seemed to sink rapidly; his feet became icy cold. I looked about for an extra covering, but could find nothing. Fortunately I had donned my winter undergarments. I stepped behind the tall headboard of the bed, and — it was an emergency, remember that, Olive, an emergency! — and divested myself of my flannel petticoat. In this garment I enveloped the young man's feet, rubbing them at the same time with all my strength. At this critical moment Dr. Robinson returned and lent his assistance. The young man recovered. He is at this moment in Thornham. He is the new minister of St. John's."

Miss Kizzy paused, overcome with emotion, and blew her bossy nose.

Olive continued to gaze at her, expectantly.

"Think of it!" Madame de Jolibois went on, lifting her clasped hands. " Think of it! The pedal extremities of a strange young man enfolded in my flannel garment!"

"But dear Miss Kizzy!" remonstrated Olive, divided between a feeling of disappointment and a desire to laugh, "if the man was unconscious, he could know nothing about it; besides" —

"What *he* thinks is of no consequence," interrupted the dancing-mistress. "It is the just resentment of Monshur *dee* Jollyboys that appalls me. The doctor may have mentioned the fact to the interesting young man, — I admit that he *is* interesting. The young man may speak of it to some imprudent member of his congregation. Monshur *dee* Jollyboys may hear of it! If Monshur *dee* Jollyboys hears of it, I fear there will be bloodshed. Monshur *dee* Jollyboys is a husband, and not even the sacred calling of the Reverend Mark Kennison can save him from the marital wrath of an injured consort. It is time you were going, child," she added, with a sudden return to her ordinary brisk tone of voice; "Betty will be getting anxious. Where is your shawl? You wore none! What imprudence! Wait, I will get Serena's nubia."

She bustled away, amid Olive's protests, and presently reappeared with a scarlet worsted, home-knitted scarf, which she wound about the girl's shoulders. "Now, then, run along," she ordered authoritatively; "I will recall Serena."

They walked across the yard together. Around a corner of the kitchen, they saw Miss Dibbs. She was hovering over a wheelbarrow, from which a tall, ungainly, whity-brown fowl was pecking some grains of corn. Her large flabby face expressed delight, not unmingled with apprehension. Alexander H. Stephens was plainly making preparations to crow. He stretched his long neck upward, and lifted his stumpy wings. There was a flapping sound, followed by an unearthly "*yawp!*" and then a small whirlwind of dust, in the midst of which Mr. Stephens's yellow legs beat the air helplessly, as he writhed on his back at Miss Serena's feet.

"He is a most remarkable biped," observed Madame de Jolibois absently, as she moved on. "Yes, there will be bloodshed, Olive, for Monshur *dee* Jollyboys is a *husband*."

Olive unlatched the little side gate, and stepped into the open common which stretched between the Dibbs freehold and Roseneath; her restrained laughter, girlish, gay, and musical, broke forth as she flew along the brown path like a swallow, her bare head dipped forward, and the long ends of the scarf floating behind her like a pair of scarlet wings.

Vanborough Herring's daughter had far outstripped her childhood's promise of beauty. The reddish-brown ringlets had given place to a crown of dusky braids, with glints of gold in their curling ends; the level eyebrows and the long lashes shading the shining eyes, with their frank, virginal expression, had darkened; the pale oval of the cheeks was touched with a faint and exquisite color; there were adorable dimples in the corners of the expressive mouth; the round white throat sloping away from the chin softened its somewhat too severe outlines; the slim, erect figure had the supple grace of a wild-wood sapling. The sorrows which had touched her young life had left a certain questioning wistfulness at times in the girl's face; but the healthful joy of living pervaded her whole being; it radiated from her like an atmosphere, and wrought consciously upon those about her. Even the stern set face of her father relaxed at her approach. More successful than ever, more publicly honored, if privately censured, his whole thought seemed now to be centred in the welfare and happiness of this last remaining scion of his house. She was rarely out of his sight. Her fearlessness in his presence, her open admiration of him, the gay *camaraderie* of her attitude toward him, contrasted curiously with the silent and shrinking devotion offered him of late years by his wife and oldest son.

Mrs. Hopson's place as housekeeper and guardian had not been filled. Liberty and Betty, relieved of all other duties, were charged with the sole care of the young mistress, whom they adored. The latter, clumsy of speech but deft of finger, and full of motherly wisdom, guarded her nursling with jealous solicitude. Liberty attended her on her walks and drives, swelling with pride in the importance of his position.

It was her father's wish that the young heiress should take her place as chatelaine of Roseneath, at the expiration of the year of mourning; and already workmen were busy renovating the red-brick mansion, and putting the half-neglected grounds in order.

"So soon?" breathed Olive, with her head on her father's shoulder. "My mother" —

"Your mother would have wished it," her father said, the muscles of his face twitching painfully.

"Van Herrin' has plum fergot the tradegy sent on him fer his sins less 'n a year ago," said Badgett, wagging his head dismally. "But jest you wait! The jedgment o' God ain't done a-strikin' him yit!"

Even June Badgett, however, forgot his evil prognostications when Van Herring's daughter smiled frankly at him. And when, one day, in passing the Man-Fig, she paused to shake his hand, and say in her clear low voice, "That was a gallant charge at Malvern Hill, where you were wounded, Mr. Badgett! I wish I had been there," — he was so overcome that he wished his Maker would strike him stone dead if he ever said anything ag'in' Van Herrin' again, bless her soft eyes!

But habit in a man verging upon sixty is too strong to be broken by the smile of a girl!

"I ought not to have stayed so long. I ought to have told Liberty to come and fetch me home," murmured Olive, glancing at the sunset sky as she sped homeward. "Papa will be uneasy; and oh, how Maum Betty will scold!" She laughed gayly; then she stood suddenly still, paralyzed with terror. The black mass thundering upon her was Balder, the great vicious bull which belonged to her father. He had escaped, somehow, from the pasture, and his eyes, as he rushed about the common, tearing up the earth and shaking his tremendous horns in the air, had caught the red gleam of the scarf floating from her shoulders! He lunged toward her, bellowing and snorting. Her feet, heavy as lead in the path, refused to obey her volition; her arms dropped helplessly; she shuddered, closing her eyes. A swift vision shot across her brain of her father awaiting her in the dim library; of Van and herself at play under the orange-trees at the " other house; " of her mother's white face on the coffin pillow! She felt upon her eyelids the dust thrown up by the infuriated animal.

A startled cry resounded on the air; and she felt herself caught up and swept from her feet. A confused noise and a volley of shouts and imprecations filled her terrified ears. She opened her eyes to find the face of Duncan Jeffrey close to her own, as he bore her, running, toward the park-gate of Roseneath. A glance back over his shoulder showed her the towering form of Liberty swaying from side to side in a titanic wrestle with the bellowing brute.

This is what had happened. Jeffrey, lurking about the neighborhood of the Dancing-Academy, for reasons best known to himself, had seen Olive come out of the side gate and start homeward. Following her at a little distance with the intention of joining her, yet strangely timorous at the thought, he had seen her danger, and had reached her barely in time to snatch her from under the very horns of the maddened beast. But it was Liberty — sent in quest of her by Betty — rushing behind him, who had thrown his own huge bulk in front of them both and seized the bull — literally by the horns.

"*Run, Mars Dunc, run! Fer Gawd-a-mighty's sake, run!*" shouted the negro, jerked from his feet and tossed backward and forward, but keeping his grip with grim determination.

It seemed a long time, but it was the work

of a moment for Jeffrey to dart with his light burden across the intervening space and reach the large gate. It swung open at his approach, and he laid the half-unconscious girl in the arms of the man who sprang forward to receive her, and turned back, running at the top of his speed. As he approached the struggling dust-enveloped mass from which hoarse roars, human and brute, arose together, Liberty got a "purchase," as he afterward expressed it, on the wide horns, and gave them a powerful sidewise wrench, which broke the creature's neck.[1] It plunged forward suddenly, and fell, a mighty lifeless heap on the trodden turf.

"'Fo' Gawd, Mars Dunc," the black giant said, wiping the perspiration from his forehead and drawing a deep breath, "I feels like I been havin' a tussle wi' ole Satan his-se'f! He was a fine bull, Balder was, an' he had de strenk o' de debble! You ain' come too soon ter save little Miss, Mars Dunc!"

The young man grasped the negro's dusty hand in his. "Good God, Lib," he cried hoarsely, "what would have become of her if it had not been for *you!*"

<hr>

[1] A fact.

Olive leaned, trembling, against the arm which sustained her, watching with horror-stricken eyes the scene on the common.

" Do not be alarmed, Miss Herring," said a grave and gentle voice; " no one is hurt, I am sure, and you see that the animal can do no more mischief."

Even in the midst of her agitation, the girl was aware of a curious thrill. No one had ever called her Miss Herring before! She blushed and looked hastily up. Her glance encountered a pair of dark serious eyes which were bent kindly upon her. Their owner, a man whose grave and somewhat careworn face belied the youthfulness of his figure, smiled upon her reassuringly. There was a hint of condescension in his tone as he said : —

"I am Mark Kennison, your rector. I had just been to call on your father. You had a narrow escape," he continued, looking over to where Jeffrey and the negro still stood beside their prostrate foe. " I saw it all, and I " — Speech suddenly failed him, as he noted clearly for the first time the features uplifted to his own. He drew the girl's hand through his arm — for she was still faint and trembling — without another word, and led her along the darkening avenue to the house. She walked silently beside him, Miss Kizzy's grotesque story struggling confusedly in her mind with an odd sense of gratitude toward this stranger who — had he saved her life? " No, it was Duncan who saved me! " she said to herself. " *Duncan!* " she repeated. Yet the feeling, in spite of herself, remained, which gave to Mark Kennison the place, momentarily at least, which of right belonged to the friend of her childhood. Curiously enough, her father, who heard the story in grim silence, involuntarily shared this feeling. He wrung the hand of the young minister, a few broken words of thanks escaping his pale lips. Kennison disclaimed any share in Olive's rescue from peril, eagerly recounting the part played therein by Jeffrey and Liberty, both unknown to him even by name.

Nevertheless, when Duncan, a little later, made his appearance, followed by Lib, he found himself relegated to the background. Olive, indeed, met him with outstretched hands, and his former colonel, less reserved with him than with the rest of the world, thanked him warmly. But something —

somehow — was lacking. The young planter stood for a moment irresolute, his honest blue eyes clouding, as he glanced from his own dusty and disordered dress to the parson's trim and elegant figure; then, with a hasty and awkward adieu, he went away.

Kennison remained to the late dinner, — one of the institutions at Roseneath much disapproved of by Thornham in general, and the Man-Fig Conclave in particular, — and spent the evening with Miss Herring and her father on the moonlighted veranda.

That night Liberty, whose exploit was the wonder and admiration of the Quarters, and who had no cause to complain of luke-warmness on the part of his beloved mistress, or the master, stood thoughtfully gazing up at the ceiling after he and Betty had retired to the privacy of their own cabin.

"What you doin', Lib?" queried Betty from the four-post bed in the corner.

"I 'm kiverin' up de fire, honey," he replied, without moving.

"Dass a lie, Lib, an' you knows it! What you got in dat woolly haid o' yo'n?"

"I 'm gwine ober in my min'," returned

Lib slowly, " de recollections of de way you shuck me when you was a gal, fer dat no-count Baptiss preacher, Jack Yates."

" Lawd, Lib," giggled Betty, among her pillows, " I did 'n keer nothin' 'bout Jack Yates! I was jis *a-tryin' you !*"

" *Is dat so?* " And Liberty's solemn face relaxed into a relieved smile.

In the great house, Big Hannah, Betty's oldest daughter, who slept on the floor in her young mistress's room, was also awake and pondering.

" I ain' never seen Miss Olive restless in her sleep befo'," she reasoned, " an' it 's de fus time Mars Dunc Jeffrey ever rid away from dis house widout stayin' fer dinner. *An' dat preacher-man is mighty good-lookin' !* "

VII.

Rose, the motherless daughter of Rufe
Drennon, had kept pace with Olive Herring
in her development into womanhood. Small
and graceful in figure, with innocent blue
eyes, a profusion of ashen-blonde hair, and
a round infantile face, she presented a striking contrast in appearance to the heiress of
Roseneath; and there were those in the
village who thought the common laborer's
only child far more attractive than her
patrician friend.

For, the two girls, after Olive's vigorous
championship of Rose at the dancing-school,
became at once inseparable. Through the
thoughtful generosity of Mrs. Herring, the
little "poor-white" shared all the advan-
tages possessed by that lady's own children.
Punctually every morning, from the cabin
on the outskirts of the town, where Drennon
lived, the child made her appearance at
Roseneath. There, in the airy schoolroom,

season after season, the youthful pair
studied from the same books, — the reddish-brown curls and the blonde locks in-
termingled ; they bewailed together the
stony-heartedness of successive governesses,
drawing and music masters ; they listened
together to Liberty's stories of the war ; and
to Betty's wonderful "ghos'" tales ; together
they were instructed in the mysteries of the
still-room by Aunt Patty Hopson, — romping and frolicking between whiles about the
shaded grounds and through the mazy rose-
garden in company with Young Van and
Duncan Jeffrey.

Rufe Drennon's dull eyes gleamed with a
sort of torpid pride when he saw his child
hand in hand with the daughter of Van
Herring. He was, himself, thus relieved
of all paternal responsibility, more stolidly
shiftless than ever, loafing from day's end
to day's end under the Man-Fig, while a
" hired nigger " (paid by Mrs. Herring)
looked after the cabin in the midst of its unkempt bit of field. Small wonder that Rose
— sweet and shallow Rose ! with her inher-
ited indolence, and her cultivated sense of refinement — should, as she grew older, spend
more and more of her time at Roseneath.

After his wife's death, Herring continued without question her lavish bounty toward her *protégée*. And so it was that a stranger happening upon them would have supposed Rose, as well as Olive, a daughter of the house.

Neither had the position of Duncan Jeffrey in the household changed in all these years. An orphan with no near relative except the choleric grand-uncle, — a pioneer into the country with Steven Thornham, — the lad had found his only idea of home-life under Vanborough Herring's roof. Honest, manly, and chivalric by nature, his attitude toward the Herring children had always been that of an elder brother. For Olive, there was an added and a tenderer feeling. He had barely reached his seventh birthday when Mrs. Herring called him, one morning, into her own room, and, smiling, laid in his arms a tiny sleeping creature who sighed contentedly as her dark head fell against his shoulder. A curious sensation stirred the boy, — forgotten immediately, but remembered and felt again the day when, smarting under Madame de Jolibois's stern reproof, he had heard his little playfellow's whispered words of praise ; remembered, and never lost sight of again. He had long called the feeling by its true name. "*I love her*," he said to himself, springing into battle at the head of his company, or trudging, a barefoot soldier, about the frozen roads of Virginia. "*I love her*," he murmured, looking up from his books at midnight in his college dormitory ; the phrase broke involuntarily from his lips beneath the shadow of old-world monuments, or in presence of storied works of art. "Does she love me?" The question must needs shake his soul, but the time was not yet.

When Uncle Billy Duncan — scarred veteran of three wars — died, soon after the boys in gray came marching home, his grand-nephew and sole heir succeeded to his fine estate, impaired, but not materially, by the war. A couple of years spent in study, another in foreign travel, and the young ex-officer settled at Good Luck, his plantation, and threw himself with ardor into its management.

Good Luck, with its outstretching cane-fields, lay on the west bank of the river, a few miles above Thornham. Its owner, as he rode thitherward in the falling dusk, after his meeting with the new Rector of St. John's, was grimly thoughtful.

" Why have I waited?" he asked himself savagely; " why, — when for years I have had the sanction of both her father and mother!   Why have I not spoken?   What a fool, an idiot, I have been to hold back, thinking her still a child, and fearing lest I might frighten her!   How her eyes shone as she looked at him !   The god has come, the half-god must go !   '*Balder is dead.*'

" ' Balder the Beautiful is dead, is dead.' "

He broke into the fragment of song, laughing not too mirthfully at the whimsical association of ideas.   He sang, in a sonorous, musical baritone, another couplet of the ballad, then fell silent again.

" No, he is *not* a prig, — the Reverend Mark Kennison!" he broke out aloud, answering some rising thought within; " he is an agreeable, manly fellow, and remarkably handsome."

This last reflection provoked a sigh which was superfluous.   For the speaker could have given odds to most men on the score of good looks.   He was somewhat above the common height, with a finely proportioned figure, which was at once graceful and commanding. His frank expressive face, almost perfect in outline, was lighted by a pair of dark blue eyes, whose steady gaze betokened strength and sincerity of purpose; his close-cut mustache was dark-brown, but the clustering curls shading his broad forehead were yellow as spun gold. Many an old veteran of the war, who has perhaps forgotten graver things, still recalls with delight the lad "wi' yaller hair a-flyin'," with the light of the camp-fire on his bonny brow, or the smoke of battle griming his boyish face!

"Yes, he is a fine fellow, — if he *is* a preacher," he repeated emphatically.

Already the bitterness had died out of his voice; the unwonted mood had passed. But the poignant question, until that moment hardly framed, "Can I win her?" remained.

"But I *will* win her, or die," he cried fiercely, turning in at his own gate, which swung open at the sound of his horse's galloping hoofs, while from the fence half a score of pickaninnies shouted a welcome to their indulgent young master.

He laughed inwardly at his own foolish fears and misgivings, when he presented himself as usual at Roseneath the next afternoon. He found Olive and Rose in the little sitting-room with Madame de Jolibois.

"Ah, here he is!" cried Olive, her eyes sparkling, though a quiver of the lip betrayed her emotion on seeing him. "Come in, Duncan. Here is Miss Kizzy wanting to know how it all happened. And so do I. For I saw nothing but the bull."

Miss Kizzy turned pale, and her lips moved. Rose said afterward that they plainly framed *gentleman-cow!*

"I had very little to do with it," Jeffrey declared, shaking hands with his old instructress. "It was Lib who carried the day. His arms must be out of joi— "

"But *you* carried off the spoils, Duncan," interrupted Rose demurely.

They all laughed at this. Olive blushed, but kept her frank eyes on Duncan's face. His own were dropped, lest in their depths might be read the tremulous joy which still possessed him, when he remembered that he had clasped her in his arms, that her head had rested against his shoulder as he bore her toward —

"Mr. Mark Kennison."

He looked up with a sudden inward shock.

Kennison had entered the room from the library where he had been sitting with his host, and was being formally presented to Rose.

The young men shook hands cordially, Duncan's momentary confusion passing like a cloud before the open greeting of the stranger. Kennison looked with vaguely puzzled eyes at Madame de Jolibois, who, sitting bolt upright on the sofa, acknowledged the introduction with a dignified bow. The talk ran for a few moments upon the adventure of the day before, then Olive, who was beginning to tremble nervously over the recollection of her danger, changed its current by turning to Miss Kizzy and inquiring —

" How is Alexander H. Stephens ? "

" He has ceased forever to crow," Miss Kizzy returned solemnly. " Serena is profoundly affected. We think it was too much corn."

Kennison looked mystified.

" Oh, I am so sorry," said Olive hysterically.

Jeffrey swallowed a laugh. " And the Academy, Miss Kizzy?" he asked. " I hope the boys have improved since my time."

"Your deportment — even as a very young gentleman — was always excellent, Duncan," replied Madame de Jolibois politely. "You will be interested to learn, my dear," she added, turning to Olive, "that we have decided upon employing an assistant. A most momentous decision." She shook her head gravely.

"Indeed!" said Olive with lively sympathy; "whom have you chosen?"

"Sarah Ann Hunter, — one of our graduates who does not wish to be entirely dependent upon her friends for her support."

Madame de Jolibois, as she said this, looked severely at Rose, of whom she distinctly disapproved. But Rose smiled so innocently that Miss Kizzy was beguiled into smiling back at her.

"Serena will continue to play the piano," she added, "and I shall of course teach grace and deportment as heretofore, during the enforced absence of Monshur dee Jollyboys. When he returns we will doubtless make other arrangements."

She arose to take her leave. A half-smile of recognition came into the rector's eyes; he held out his hand and opened his lips to speak; but the old lady drew back with a

stiff Dancing-Academy "curchey" and went
away, followed by Jeffrey and Olive, who
walked with her to her own gate. There
she waved the young man aside, and drawing Olive to her she whispered tragically,
"He possesses the dangerous secret, Olive,
my child. I saw it in his visual orbs. I
fear there will be bloodshed."

The two young people walked back across
the common, laughing a little at Miss Kizzy's
delusions, then dropping into silence. The
girl seemed constrained and preoccupied,
and her companion, with beating heart, was
vainly trying to formulate some indifferent
remark concerning the new minister, when
she stopped abruptly. It was upon the spot
— still showing signs of the conflict in the
beaten grass and plowed soil — where, not
twenty-four hours earlier, her life had been
for a moment in deadly peril.

"I can see those horrible flaming eyes
yet," she said in an awed tone; "O Duncan, how can I thank you! how can I ever
repay you!"

For all answer, he caught her hand, and a
torrent of words came struggling to his lips.

"Olive! Duncan!" called Rose in her
shrill sweet voice. He looked up. She was

coming down the avenue of oaks to meet them, accompanied by Mark Kennison.

.   .   .   .

Thus was added, almost without the formality of an introduction, a new element to the intimate life of Roseneath.

The young clergyman, while instituting energetic changes in his church, — changes somewhat startling to his conservative congregation, — still had leisure to enter with zest into his novel and attractive surroundings.   Born in a colder climate and among a more reserved people, Mark Kennison's fervid and poetic temperament found something curiously akin to itself in the rose-gardens and orange-groves; the stately many-galleried houses; the joyous open-air life and warm responsiveness of this far-away little Southern town.

" How did you happen to come so far away from home, Mr. Kennison ? " demanded Rose one afternoon when the now familiar quartette lingered together on the front gallery, watching the brown patched sails on a schooner creep down the river.

" So far away from home ! " echoed Kennison dreamily; " it was rather the return of an exile ! "   His eyes as he spoke met those of Olive Herring turned curiously toward him. A quick flush passed over his swarthy cheek. "I came," he continued in a conventional tone, "to accompany a sick friend to San Antonio. On my homeward journey I stopped in H——, where I was caught by the yellow-fever epidemic just then breaking out. I had the fever myself, and when the quarantine was raised, my strength was too exhausted to permit me at once to return to my duties. I therefore resigned my former charge and returned to San Antonio. There I received the call to St. John's — where " — He paused, his eyes wandering absently over the soft October landscape.

"Where, may you wave forever!" concluded Rose irreverently.

"Amen!" ejaculated Jeffrey in the same tone, looking up from the Lamarque rose-vine which with Liberty's help he was training about one of the fluted pillars of the veranda.

"How still the air is!" said Olive, rising and strolling down the steps.

.   .   .   .

"Sho's you bawn, Betty," Lib declared that night at the usual hour for such confidences, "ef Mars Dune don't hump his-se'f, he 's gwine ter lose de race!"

"Why 'nt he hump his-se'f, den?" cried Betty indignantly. "Ef Mars Dune don't keer enough fer Miss Olive ter head off dat preacher-man, den let de preacher-man git her. Dass de way wi' man-folks, anyhow. So biggaty, dey think a gal is boun' fer ter drop in dey mouth lak a briled pattridge! Lawd, ef Miss Olive has got de right sort o' *spunk*, she 's gwine ter hol' dat preacher-man over Mars Dune's haid lak I helt Jack Yates over yo'n, ontell " —

"Shet up, gal, an' go to sleep," interrupted Lib with a smothered chuckle. "I got to 'scort dem young folks up to Good Luck to-morrow to see de sugar-bilin'."

.   .   .   .

The Herring carriage, drawn by its sleek bays, and driven by Liberty in person, stopped the next morning about ten o'clock in front of the rambling plantation-house at Good Luck. Mrs. Huddlestone, fat and motherly, came bustling down the steps to receive the visitors as they alighted.

"Lord, honey, how you 've grown!" she cried, bestowing a sounding kiss upon Olive's cheek. "And I do declare you 're the mortal

spi't of your cousin, Elinor Thornham!
How 's the Colonel? Well an' hearty?"

Mrs. Huddlestone dated back to the very
earliest days of Thornham. She had been
Major Billy Duncan's housekeeper at Good
Luck for more than thirty years, and continued to perform that important service for
his grand-nephew.

"And bless my soul, Rose Drennon, if you
ain't got on long dresses! How 's yo' paw,
honey? I ain't seen Rufe Drennon for a
coon's age!" Her tone, though still kindly,
became slightly patronizing as she addressed
the girl who belonged to her own class.
"You 'll find Mr. Duncan over at the sugar-
house," she went on, waddling across the
house-yard in front of the party, "onless
you come into the dinin'-room an' have
some buttermilk, first? It 's just out o' the
churn. You don't keer for it? Well. Here,
Jupe, you lazy, good-for-nothing limb o'
Satan, run ahead an' open the gates for yo'
Miss Olive. Look out for them tie-vines,
honey." This last admonition was addressed
to Kennison, who stared and blushed a little
at the familiarity; but recovered himself
when he heard her say to the setter trotting
beside her, as she turned toward the house:

"Now, Alamo, honey, ain't you ashamed o' yo'self to be a-barkin' at Lib Thornham like as if you had n't never set eyes on him afore!"

Jupe, coal-black, plump and ragged, raced across the wide grassy lot, bursting with vain-glory, and swung open the large gate leading into a rose-hedged lane, beyond which towered the great square red-brick chimneys of the sugar-house. From these a circling column of velvety-black smoke wavered upward. Below stretched the broad low expanse of the sugar-shed. High-wheeled wagons drawn by sturdy sugar mules were lumbering in, loaded with purplish-red and golden-yellow cane ; their grinning drivers shouted and gesticulated at the occupants of the empty carts clattering back to the fields. A file of men alongside the creeping "carrier" were feeding it steadily from the huge pile of cane hard by. Clouds of white steam blew out at intervals from the engines whose regular pulses throbbed noisily. A small mountain of *bagasse* arose in the rear of the shed ; over against it a row of discarded sugar-kettles showed their flaring sides, red with rust. The wholesome smell of boiling cane-juice was everywhere.

The young planter came across the busy inclosure to greet his guests. His hat was pushed back from his forehead and he was in his shirt-sleeves. He excused himself for not having been at the house to meet them on their arrival.

"We were tinkering upon a piece of broken shafting. Welcome to Good Luck," he said, shaking hands heartily with Kennison. "It has been two years since you were here," he continued, speaking to the two girls, but looking at Olive. "I have made a great many improvements since. Will you go over the sugar-house, first? Or shall we see the cane-cutting?"

"The cane-cutting first," decided Rose, who was scampering about, heedless and joyous as a young kitten.

Jeffrey gave some instructions to his manager, then, drawing on his coat, he led the way to the fields, which, blue-green and billowy under the morning sun, made a smiling background in every direction for the central picture of noise and activity.

It was Kennison's first view of a sugar plantation, and he looked about him with keen interest.

The autumn day was perfect; the sky

was absolutely cloudless, except where the vapory smoke from the sugar-house chimneys banked itself against the eastern horizon. A soft breeze stirred the tall cane, which moved with an incessant murmurous rustling. The broad ditches intersecting the fields were ablaze with ragged sunflowers and wide-disked coreopsis; the grass, still green underfoot, was sprinkled with coarse purple daisies.

The smell of honeysuckle and roses intermixed came in whiffs from the dooryards of the Quarter, whose cabins stood in a double row to the right of the open lane. From "Indian-cut," — so named from a low mound marking its boundary — where the cane-cutters were at work, a chorus, monotonous, plaintive, weird, arose and floated away to lose itself in the outlying swamps. As Jeffrey and his friends drew nearer the words were distinguishable: —

"Stan' right still, an' steady yo'se'f,
Sinner!
Zoom-ba-loom-ba!
De Lawd gwine ter move dis Ark His-se'f,
Sinner!
Zoom-ba-loom-ba!
Look to de eas' an' look to de wes',
Sinner!
Zoom-ba-loom-ba!

De saints o' de Lawd marchin' abreas',
Zoom-ba-loom-ba!
Zoom!"

The song ceased abruptly, and the singers greeted the master with a lusty shout. The gang numbered about one hundred, of whom nearly one half were women, — strong, stalwart, and brawny, — their striped turbans and blue skirts distinguishing them from their male companions. The cutters moved with swift rhythmic step among the cane; the broad, keen-edged, hooked knives rose and fell in unison, stripping the leaves, and severing the stalks with unerring precision.

A bent and wrinkled old negro on horseback, who was directing their movements, rode forward and dismounted, baring his gray head.

Jeffrey nodded pleasantly. "Well, Jerry," he said, "how is your gang working to-day?"

"Pretty well, Mars Dunc, pretty well, sah," returned the old man. "Injun-cut's nigh erbout finished, sah." He pointed with his whip, as he spoke, to the denuded portion of the field, where the cane lay right and left, alternately, across the furrows in symmetrical heaps, the stripped stalks glistening in the sun.

"Very well, Uncle Jerry," commented his master with a smile of approval, "come up to the house to-night, and I 'll see what I can do for you."

Jerry ducked his head, snickering into his hat. He felt in anticipation a finger of Mars Dunc's mellow Bourbon slipping like perfumed oil down his dry old throat.

He swung himself lightly into the saddle and resumed his wonted air of severe disapproval.

The planter, walking back across the field, explained to Kennison, excited and enthusiastic, the methods of planting and cultivating the cane.

" It is not without its compensations, life on a sugar plantation," he concluded, "but it is from year's end to year's end; it is a constant financial risk, and it is monotonous."

"I should never tire of it," declared Olive with conviction.

Duncan's heart gave a sudden leap, and his eyes lighted as if the hope of a lifetime were already realized. He could hardly trust himself to look at her. When he did steal a glance in her direction, her calmly unconscious face sobered him, and his momentary elation died away.

Far behind them the chorus of the cane-cutters again filled the air with its curious meaningless refrain : —

> " Zoom-ba-loom-ba !
> Zoom ! "

After the noontide rest, spent in loitering about the cabins and offices, they inspected the sugar-making. It was in the days of the open kettles ; the ponderous and wonderful machinery of the present time had not yet been introduced, and the process was more simple, more wasteful, and more picturesque. When they had seen it all, from the sickly, sweetish, green juice, pouring from the crushers, to the great vats of dark, slowly-cooling molasses, and the moist heaps of yellow sugar, — shoveled like golden sand from the clean floors and thrown, spadeful by spadeful, into the waiting barrels, — they came out and stood by the carrier, watching its slow upward movement. The feeders were mostly negroes ; but there were two white men among them ; an old " poor-white," with a long lean patient face, who stooped painfully over his work; and a young man whose black eyes glowed dully beneath scowling brows. The latter, whose name was Hogan, worked at the upper end of the carrier. He stepped to the ever-lessening, always-growing pile of cane, and slowly pulled from it an armful of stalks, staring boldly the while at the two pretty young women. Turning to the man who stood next him, he said something in a low tone, lifting his load at the same time to cast it into the carrier. As he did so he stumbled, and the cane, missing its mark, fell to the ground. Jeffrey, who had lingered a moment in the sugar-house, had come out unobserved; and as the man recovered himself he sprang at him without a word and dealt him a blow with his clenched fist full upon the mouth. Hogan dropped like a stone, but rose immediately, the blood streaming from his face, and looked around him with glaring eyeballs. When he recognized his antagonist, however, he stooped, muttering sullenly, and began to pick up the scattered cane.

The negroes stopped work for a second, and a smothered laugh of approval passed along the line. Kennison looked pained and surprised; Rose drew timidly back; Olive's eyes blazed with indignation.

Jeffrey wiped the blood from his hand with his handkerchief. "Here comes Jupe to say that dinner is waiting," he said in his ordinary tone. "I hope that you all have a country appetite."

Olive walked beside him in displeased silence, her lips quivering and her cheeks flushed.

"Was not that rather a severe punishment for so trifling an offense as dropping an armful of cane?" she demanded in a low tone, when she could sufficiently command her voice.

"Perhaps," he answered good-humoredly, though he winced a little. "But discipline is necessarily severe on the plantation during sugar-making time."

The Good Luck plantation-house was a wide-galleried one-story structure, which "spraddled," as Mrs. Huddlestone said, "all over creation." The late Major Duncan, who had remained a bachelor all his life, had followed his own whims in the matter of building, undeterred by the mild remonstrances of his housekeeper, constructing wings, adding closets, throwing out porches, as their need became apparent. The result was quaintly pleasing to the eye. There was a certain bareness within; the large rooms, containing only the necessary pieces of ponderous old-fashioned furniture, lacked the dainty touch of a woman's hand. This in itself was a constant source of inward gratification to the present owner. "It will be Olive," — he said it shyly to himself, — "it will be Olive who will make the old place look like home!"

The banks of the river, which made a long outward curve in front of the plantation, were lower here than at Thornham. The windows of the dining-room looked directly out upon La Salle Point, the place where the famous French explorer was reputed to have made his crossing on that last fatal journey in search of the Chevalier Tonti, which ended in his death. Through the noble trees which studded the park, glimpses of the yellow water could be seen. On the further side, a bit of unbroken forest stretched away to the horizon.

"Dinner's ready," announced Mrs. Huddlestone, appearing on the gallery where the party was enjoying this view. "You set at the head of the table, honey," she whispered to Olive, "an' keep yo' eye on them keerless dinin'-room boys. Lib Thornham's in the pantry, an' I'm goin' to stay in the kitchen. Lord, I hope young Mr. Duncan will be satisfied!"

There was no ground for complaint. The late William Duncan, variously known as "Major" and "Uncle Billy" Duncan, had been a notoriously good liver, and he had left behind him a cook who had been for years the envy of his neighbors.

The behavior of "the boys," a couple of sedate middle-aged men, under Liberty's severe supervision, was admirable; nothing was lacking in the appointment of the table with its handsome hereditary service of silver and glass. Yet — the dinner was not a success.

The master of Good Luck, who had been planning and arranging for weeks, and who had looked forward with almost feverish impatience to seeing Olive Herring at the head of his own dinner-table, confessed to himself with a sinking heart that things somehow had gone wrong. A constraint was upon them all. Kennison indeed talked, but the heartiness of his tone was gone; Olive was cold and unresponsive; even

Rose, looking with questioning eyes from one to another, was silent.

It was a relief when they rose at last from the table. Almost immediately the carriage appeared at the door, for the afternoon shadows were beginning to fall.

"Come again soon, honey," Mrs. Huddlestone called from the head of the steps. Jeffrey, leaning against the wheel, longed but did not dare to echo her invitation. He looked somewhat wistfully at them all.

"I shall not be able to be much at Roseneath until the grinding is over," he said, stepping back after the adieux were said.

The carriage rolled away. He watched it until a turn in the road hid it from sight. The smile that curved his lips was tinged with bitterness. But his voice was cheery enough as he called up to his housekeeper, lifting his hat, "Thank you, Mrs. Huddlestone! The dinner would have delighted Uncle Billy himself."

He walked rapidly to the sugar-house, where the night-torches were already flaring; the smoke from the huge chimney was starred with red sparks; the engines pounded ceaselessly; the figures moving about in the purple gloom, carrying lanterns, had a ghostly look; in the little upper room where the chemist tested the "takes," a greenish light glittered like a planet; the feeders along the carrier were droning a mournful hymn.

At the gate leading into the inclosure, Jeffrey encountered the man, Hogan. He stopped and regarded him for a moment with lips compressed and fingers itching.

"You scoundrel! you — you cowardly hound!" he said when he could speak. "How dare you show yourself to me! Leave this place instantly; and if I ever catch you on my premises again, I will break every bone in your body!"

Before he had finished speaking, Hogan had slunk away.

This is what Jeffrey had overheard earlier in the day when he came up unseen behind the man: —

"*Hmp!* Van Herrin's pretty gal looks stuck up, don't she! Wonder ef she's a thieft lak her daddy!"

VIII.

TWO CAMPAIGNS.

THAT winter was the gayest known in
Thornham since its brief reign as the capital
of an infant republic. Roseneath, whose
chatelaine for the second time in the history
of the manor-house was a beautiful and
charming young woman, continued to be, as
in times past, the focus whence radiated all
social animation. Herring, apparently absorbed in his public duties, and busied with
money speculations, yet appeared to note
with ever-increasing pride the success of the
joyous young creature who might be said to
redeem all his own past. He spared no
pains to add to her pleasures or her tri-
umphs. There were no more quiet expedi-
tions to Good Luck plantation, where the
grinding of an enormous crop went on un-
interruptedly; but there was a succession
of plantation parties at Fair View, — parties which brought together people from
all quarters of the country, and which

were veritable fairy-tales of mirth and extravagance.

Jeffrey — the press of the sugar-making over — took his wonted place as leader in this gay circle, the momentary constraint which followed his unexplained and apparently unjustifiable assault on the man Hogan quite forgotten by his friends at Roseneath.

Kennison's advent, too, had awakened a lively, and, truth to tell, half-puzzled interest throughout the little town. His magnetism in the pulpit swept his listeners with enthusiasm with ritualistic changes and exterior reforms, which in cooler moments they did not sanction; his free association with what Miss Kizzy called the Realm of Fashion was sharply criticised and denounced by the older members of St. John's; but even these melted into smiling approval before his winning and sympathetic personality.

"I wish my Maker may strike me stone dead ef the parson ain't a plum out-'n-out gentleman," was June Badgett's verdict. For Kennison, doubly interested in this group of men, as souls oftentimes awry, and as types hitherto unknown to his experience, often stopped under the Man-Fig and talked familiarly with the Council.

To Vanborough Herring, whose scholarly instincts in rare moments asserted themselves before the lettered young divine and met with quick and tactful response, he stood nearer than any man — except perhaps Duncan Jeffrey — had stood for many years.

The rush went bravely on. In the midst of it Herring announced himself as a candidate for the United States Congress. His election was a foregone conclusion; nevertheless the campaign, which was a vigorous one, necessitated frequent absences from home, and a breathless coming and going of party leaders and political subalterns.

Almost at the moment of this announcement, the small world of Thornham awoke, electrified, to the fact that another, and to the isolated and self-centred community a far more important campaign was in progress in their midst. The dullest eye in the village could be no longer blind to the certainty that the Rector of St. John's and the master of Good Luck plantation were open and determined, though friendly rivals for the favor of Olive Herring.

Public sentiment was divided between the two suitors. There was scarcely a man or woman in the county who had not known and loved Duncan Jeffrey from his freckle-faced and awkward, but always honest and loyal boyhood, to the present moment. But the glamour of romance was on the side of the stranger.

"Of course she will marry Duncan!" said Madame de Jolibois confidently; "she would not be so foolish as to — Why, he toted her when she was a baby, and made mud-pies for her, when " —

"Fiddlesticks, Keziah," interrupted Mrs. Alsbury, who was arguing the case with her. "Olive Herring is just as wise and no wiser than other girls. She 'll marry the preacher's dark eyes, and you 'll live to see it."

"Vanborough Herring's daughter?" said an eminent statesman — a keen, subtle, observant man of the world — who had spent some days at Fair View in conference with the congressional candidate. "She is simply *living*. Every fibre of her beautiful young body is alive; every sense is alert. But she has, as yet, learned neither to feel nor to think. When that time comes, the man who wins her will indeed be a fortunate one!"

The object of this solicitous interest meanwhile maintained an unconscious girlish dignity which made any allusion to the subject impossible in her presence. Liberty and Betty continued to discuss it hotly in the privacy of their own cabin.

" Why 'nt Mars Dunc hump his-se'f ! " Betty would cry wrathfully. " Is he gwine ter give dat preacher-man a walk-over ? "

And Liberty, from the book of his own experience, would reply, " Lawd, gal, Mars Dunc neenter fret. He kin come in on de home-stretch. *He ain' ham-strenk yit*, bless Gawd ! "

Thus the two campaigns went on side by side, the air fairly throbbing with anticipation and excitement. The conclusion of the political contest in Herring's triumphant elevation to the coveted seat at Washington was inevitable.

But the result of the sentimental tourney remained doubtful.

IX

THE PALM-TREE GIRL.

"Where is Liberty, Maum Betty?" asked Miss Herring one afternoon, putting her head in at the summer-house door.

Betty looked up from the bench where she was sitting with a heaped-up tray of violets on her lap.

"Lib?" — she stopped to chuckle softly to herself, — "dat fool nigger, Miss Olive, has gone to 'Mancipation."

"Sure enough, this is Emancipation Day! I had forgotten. That is why the place is so quiet. Why did you not go yourself, Maum?"

"Who, me? Lawd, chile, does you think I ain' got nothin' to do but to go trailin' a'ter 'Mancipation? Ez fer Lib, he's dat narrer-minded dat he ain' 'shame to caper off de minit Mars Van gin him leave. Gawd knows what debblement dem free-niggers is up to out yander at 'Mancipation!"

"Oh, *Maum!*" the tall girl sank on her

knees beside her old nurse and caressed her shriveled hands coaxingly, "you want to go, I am sure you do! And you have been promising to take me ever since 'freedom.' Cannot we go to-day? Rose and I? And Duncan? *Please*, Maum Betty!"

Betty's eyes brightened, but she turned her head away with an affectation of reluctance. "Lawd, honey, what intrus has a grown-up young lady like you got in dem free-niggers! . . . But ef you is sot on it! . . . Dey ain' no mo' 'count dan a passel o' kerkle-burs! . . . 'Sides, I got to fix yo' vi'let-water. But ef Mars Dunc 'll go 'long " —

By this time she was urging her objections upon empty air, for Olive had sped across the rose-garden, crying with the eagerness of a child, " Rose! Rose! come!"

Half an hour later the two girls came out of the house accompanied by Jeffrey, and followed at a respectful distance by Betty, in a monstrous gala-day turban, her best bombazine gown, and white kerchief. At the foot of the steps they encountered Kennison, who turned back with them, delighted at the opportunity of witnessing the famous celebration of Emancipation Day.

[It may be explained, in passing, that the negroes in the Southern States celebrate the day upon which the proclamation reached them, and not the day upon which it was promulgated. Hence the date differs according to their nearness or remoteness from the seat of government.]

Their way led them directly past the Jolibois Dancing-Academy. The sound of shuffling feet within and the tinkle of the piano indicated that the Saturday afternoon class (an innovation by Sarah Hunter) was in training.

Olive left her companions at the gate and ran in. Madame de Jolibois sat on the high-backed sofa, with a red rose in her hair, glaring at her assistant. Sarah Hunter was hopelessly entangled with her young charges in the intricate " hands-all-around " of the Lancers. It took the visitor but a moment to unravel the chain.

" I only came in to see how you are getting on, Miss Kizzy. We are going to the Emancipation picnic," she explained, " Rose and Duncan and I — and Mr. Kennison."

Madame de Jolibois smiled affectionately up at her young friend. " Duncan Jeffrey," she remarked irrelevantly, " is the most cultivated young gentleman in Thornham, by far. I am sure that Monshur dee Jollyboys, when he returns, will approve of Duncan Jeffrey. Mr. Kennison is also highly proper," she added, with some haste. "I am satisfied, Olive," — her voice sank to a whisper, though Miss Serena's monotonous thumping and Sarah Hunter's loud commands made such a precaution unnecessary, — "I am satisfied that he has never divulged the dangerous secret. It is well. Monshur dee Jollyboys is a husband. And there would have been bloodshed."

Newall, from the open window of his office, saw them approaching, and came out to meet them. Time had borne heavily upon the lawyer; his friends often wondered why; for the income from his profession more than sufficed for his simple needs, and he had no other cares. He walked with his head down and his hands behind his back, like an old man. He was quite bald. His clothes, as usual, were well-worn and shabby. The curiously sad look in his eyes seemed out of keeping with his large features and bulky figure.

He held Olive's hand between his own while he chatted pleasantly with them; and he looked lingeringly after her as she moved away with Kennison at her side, Jeffrey and Rose walking together behind them.

"How like she is to Elinor Thornham," he muttered; "the same proud, yet sweet look; the same smile, the very same smile! Keep to the rear, Duncan, my boy," he added bitterly, "she is not for you. It is the stranger who wins now — as then."

.   .   .   .

The place chosen by the negroes for their annual gathering was about a mile distant from the straggling suburbs of the village. The level stretch of ground from which the undergrowth had been cleared away was shaded by vast live-oaks whose green was intermixed with the dusty-gray of downward-sweeping Spanish moss. There was a rude attempt at decoration above the grove; flags and streamers fluttered from poles planted in the open spaces; ropes of evergreen hung dangling between them. Near the centre of the grounds a rough platform had been erected, and scattered about under the trees were numberless little tables loaded with food and presided over by high-turbaned dames, famous in the annals of the county for their skill in cookery. A well-trodden and dusty plot in the rear was reserved for dancing. This place, however, as well as the quarter laid off for foot-races, ball-playing, and other sports, was for the moment deserted; and the large assemblage, as the party from Roseneath drew near, was pressing toward the raised platform.

Here, upon a huge split-bottomed chair ornamented with streamers of red, white, and blue calico, which stood on the dais, sat Uncle Isham Lester. His hands rested on his knees; his body was rigidly erect; his eyes were half-closed; his lips were compressed.

Uncle Isham was the " Centre Figger."

" The Centre Figger," Olive explained in a whisper to Kennison, " is the man or woman chosen each year by the negro community to preside over Emancipation Day. It is a great honor."

They had stationed themselves in the shade of a tree a little to the right of the dais, whence they could observe the proceedings. Liberty and Big Hannah greeted them, grinning, from the crowd; and Betty's younger children plunged toward her uproariously, butting a path for themselves through the swaying remonstrating throng, with their woolly heads.

"De Centre Figger is gwine to norate," announced Jack Yates, the sleek brown Baptist preacher, in a pompous tone from the steps of the platform. "De Daughters of Rebecca will percede de noration by singin' de Hymn o' Freedom. De conjugation will jine in de chorus."

The Daughters of Rebecca, a band of black but comely damsels in a grotesque uniform of blue and white paper-cambric, who were ranged behind the split-bottomed throne, broke into a wild chant as Uncle Isham rose and stepped forward : —

> "The Angull Gab'l he up an' axed de Lawd,
>   'Lawd, why 'nt you set dem colored people free ?'
>   And de Lawd he anserd, 'I 'm bidin' my time
>   Ter set my people free !
>   Free ! Free !
>   Bidin' my time
>   Ter set my people free ! ' "

The immense crowd took up the chorus :

> "Free ! Free !
>   Bidin' my time
>   Ter set my people free ! "

The drowsy summer air fairly thrilled with the volume of sound. There were those in the motley multitude — old men and women with scarred brows, whose backs had smarted under the lash — who sang the anthem with solemn fervor, the tears streaming down their black faces ; the younger ones sang it exultantly, insolently, clapping their hands and swinging their bodies to its rhythm; the children with their piping voices echoed the refrain. Louder and louder it rose ; faster and faster; the excited mass began to surge and roar like a storm-swollen sea; a subtle and penetrating odor pervaded the atmosphere. Blood-shot eyeballs rolled in the direction of the white faces turned almost awestruck upon them ; a Berserker rage was rising, blind, unreasoning, resistless!

Jeffrey, signaling to Liberty for assistance in case it was needed, was on the point of hurrying his companions away, when Uncle Isham lifted his hand. The tumultuous throng fell into instant silence.

The old man stood for a moment looking quietly but masterfully down upon the mass of faces uplifted to his own. He was very black, though his features had none of the grotesqueness of the typical negro face ; his large nose was straight, his lips curiously thin. His forehead was branded with tat-

too marks; these hieroglyphs also circled
his bare arms, and were traced diagonally
across his naked breast, — the sign of his
royal birth.   For Uncle Isham was an African prince.   One of those nameless inward-
stealing vessels which plied between the
coast of Guinea and Thornham in its early
days had set him ashore at midnight in the
canebrake with several hundred others of
his color.   He was then in the strength and
vigor of young manhood; now his head was
snow-white, and his once tall and commanding form was shrunken with age.   But his
dark eyes glowed fiercely beneath their over-
hanging brows.   There was something about
him, even under the threatening whip of the
overseer, which inspired fear and respect.
" Me slave outside," he sometimes said,
drawing himself up with truly royal dignity,
" inside, me king."

He began to speak slowly and as if mea-
suring each word.   Reduced to plain Eng-
lish, from his uncouth but musical *patois*,
his brief speech ran somewhat after this
fashion : —

" My friends, I am an old man and I
cannot talk much.   You have made me the
Centre Figger, and you have done well.

For you have been once slaves and you celebrate your freedom. But I have been twice a slave, I who am the son of a king. I, who would have been a king myself, I have been a slave to white people in this country who have been kind to me; and I have been a slave in my own country to black people who lashed my back with leather thongs. I was a prince. I lived in a great-house. I also had slaves who were as the dust under my feet. Do you think white men were the only people who had slaves? There was a wall around the king's great-house, and beyond there was a grove of palm-trees. Do you want to know how I became a slave? I will tell you. It is the first time that I have told it. There was a hut in the grove of palms. And a girl, who had brown eyes and a soft skin, came out of the hut. I saw her over the wall; and though the king, my father, had forbidden the gate to be opened, I opened it and went down to where the girl stood under the palms. Not once, but many times. And there, at last, I was seized and carried into the country of my father's enemy. And I was dust under his foot. For many years I served in his field, until the white man bought me from him, and fetched me across the big water to be the dust under his foot. Now, I am twice free, and I live in a land where there are no slaves. But something in a man dies hard."

He paused, and his uplifted arm fell to his side. When he spoke again, it was in a low dreamy tone; a strange light softened his sunken eyes.

"I have a wife," he said. "She is a good woman. She has made me a father seven times. She has planted the gourd-vine in my dooryard and kept my hearth bright. But I would be slave again to the white man who has been kind to me, and slave again to the black man who lashed the blood from my back with a leather thong; I would be chained like a dog in the dark place of the ship, burnt with fever and parched with thirst. For what? do you ask me? For a sight of the blue sky of my country? But I tell you, no. To sit beside the king, my father, on his gold-fringed mat? But I tell you, no! Twice am I free, but twice would I be a slave again to look once more in the eyes of the girl who waited for me under the palm-tree!"

This unexpected climax confused and bewildered his listeners; they gazed at each other in open-mouthed amazement. The prince had seated himself in his chair and resumed his impassive attitude. An aged negress came up out of the throng and stood beside him with her hand on his shoulder, looking down at the sea of faces with proudly defiant eyes.

It was his wife.

She opened her lips as if to speak; but the Reverend Jack Yates, recovering from his momentary stupefaction, motioned to the Daughters of Rebecca, and again the triumphant chorus swelled forth : —

> "Free ! Free !
> I 'm bidin' my time
> Ter set my people free."

" Let us go," said Jeffrey to his friends, and they slipped away unobserved. Liberty, working his way through the press, reached them as they entered the tangled glade stretching away to the edge of the town. He looked a little shamefaced as he dropped behind with Betty and the children. Big Hannah, being President of the Sisters of Deborah, had remained with that uniformed, be-streamered, and be-badged association.

"Well, Lib," said Betty quizzically, "has you got nuff o' dat free-nigger foolishness? Ef I was Unk' Is'om Lester's wife"—

"But you ain', honey!" cried Liberty, recovering his accustomed jauntiness, "you ain'. You my wife, an' my pa'm-tree gal besides; an' de onlies' woman dat I ever shined my eyes on."

The young people walked rather silently along the rutty wagon-road which threaded its way between the over-arching trees. Once or twice Kennison' stopped to pick a wild-flower, or a bit of fern; the others gazed at him as he did so with abstracted and dreamy eyes, hearing inwardly the echoes of Uncle Isham's love-story.

When they reached the outer park-gate of Roseneath, Rose stopped.

"I must go home," she said; "I cannot come in."

"Why, Rose!" remonstrated Olive.

"I promised my father that I would be there to-night. I have not seen him for a week. I must go," Rose continued with a little break in her voice, which showed how great was the sacrifice.

Olive did not urge her. For, ease-loving and shallow as the girl undoubtedly was,

she was stoutly loyal to her uncouth, slouch-
ing, idle father.

"I will come back Monday afternoon,"
she said, looking at them all as she turned
to go. Her eyes had a new wistfulness in
them; something like a dawning soul looked
out of their blue depths.

Duncan had a momentary struggle with
himself; then he stepped forward. "I will
go with you, Rose," he said. "It is too
late for you to go alone." She smiled
gratefully, and they turned down the road
in the direction of Drennon's cabin.

The low sun threw a soft glow over the
rose-garden. Kennison passed with Olive
along one of the lavender-bordered walks,
and drew her without speaking into the old
summer-house. Liberty and the children
disappeared around a corner of the gallery,
but Betty seated herself with a discontented
air on the steps.

"Lawd," she muttered, with her chin in
her hand and her scowling gaze fixed upon
the summer-house. "Why 'n't Mars Dunc
stay here an' min' his own business, stidder
takin' dat gal Rose home. I seen a look in
de preacher-man's eyes whilse Unk' Is'om
was noratin' 'bout dat pa'm-tree gal, an'

sho's you bawn he's co'tin' Miss Olive yander in de summer-house dis minit."

Betty's instincts, and her knowledge of man in his kind, had not deceived her.

"Miss Herring — Olive!" Kennison was saying in a voice shaken by emotion, "do I need to tell you that I love you? That I have looked over the wall of my every-day existence and seen you standing under the palm-trees of love! May I open the gate and come to you? Will you give me the love which I crave, Olive? Will you be my wife?"

It was but a half-whispered word which he bent to hear. But it was enough. She hid her agitated face on his shoulder, yielding as loyally to his caress as she had proudly withheld even from herself any admission of her love until openly wooed.

Nearly an hour passed in the first rapturous interchange of confidence, and mutual confession. Kennison at last arose, reluctantly, to go.

"To-morrow is Sunday," he said, "and I have still a part of my sermon to prepare. I may speak to your father soon, may I not? It will seem an eternity until I see you again!"

He came back from the gate to assure himself once more, as he laughingly said, that he had not been dreaming, and then ran, with a light and boyish step, down the road toward the town.

He was scarcely out of sight, and Olive still sat in the summer-house, where the gray twilight shadows were gathering, when Jeffrey opened the gate.

At sight of him Betty shook her head mournfully. "De winnin' hoss has done gone under de rope, Mars Dunc! You is too late!" she groaned beneath her breath, waving him silently to the summer-house.

He walked with a determined step across the rose-garden.

"Olive," he began abruptly, standing before her with bared head, "I love you. I have loved you ever since you were a baby. Will you marry me?"

His wooing was rude enough in contrast with Kennison's poetic and impassioned appeal. But it moved the girl strangely. A storm of conflicting emotions swept suddenly over her.

"O Duncan!" she cried, springing up and putting out an entreating hand. Her face was pale, and her dark eyes looked troubled in the wan light.

He caught her hand and pressed it with both his own against his breast.

"I am but a common-place fellow, Olive; I know that I do not deserve such happiness; but I would give my life for you. I will try to be worthy of you. I will study your wishes, I will" —

"Don't, Duncan," she pleaded imploringly, "I" —

The eager flush faded from his cheek.

"Is it — is it Kennison?" he asked slowly.

"Yes," she answered, trying to steady her voice, "I am going to marry Mr. Kennison."

Duncan loosed the hand he still held, then he caught it again in a firm clasp.

"He is a noble fellow, and far more worthy of you than I could ever be. God bless you, Olive; I know you will be happy!"

He lifted her hand to his lips, touched with reverent fingers her bowed head, and was gone.

.   .   .   .

Kennison's thoughts, as he bounded along the dusty road, were of so joyous a nature that he could hardly refrain from shouting them aloud for all the world to hear; already they had leaped forward with a daring which a few hours earlier he would have deemed preposterous; for he could not but realize that his rival — his equal in all other respects — was, from a worldly point of view, far better suited than himself to the future heiress of Roseneath. Now! he lifted his eyes to the distant spire of St. John's Church, touched with the last pale-gold of the evening light, and his heart beat exultantly at the inward vision which swam before them; he saw himself waiting at the altar, while up the aisle came to him, with down-dropped eyes, and fair face, shining like a star through the mist of her veil, his bride. *His bride!* He murmured the words aloud, in a sort of rapture.

Suddenly he slackened his pace, and tried to shake himself into soberness; for some one was approaching him in the falling dusk. As he drew nearer, he recognized the squat figure and red puffy face of June Badgett.

"How do you do, Mr. Badgett?" he inquired heartily, stopping to shake hands.

"Wa-al," drawled June, "I ain't over an' above well, parson. Ef I had my druthers, I'd be in bed; but I promised Mis' Alsbury, day before yistiddy, that I'd fetch her some mint-'n'-tansy; an' I reckin she's in a swivet to git it before supper."

He laughed lazily, shifting the basket of herbs from one arm to the other.

"You have not been to church for a long time, Badgett," — Kennison vainly tried to throw some severity into his voice.

"Lord, parson, I can't do everything an' go to mill, too," cried June. "'Pears like some folks kin, — 'specially ef they start out by stealin' di'mon's." He pointed his elbow significantly, as he spoke, at Herring, who flashed by in a light buggy drawn by a pair of superb horses.

"Eh? What did you say, Badgett?" asked Kennison abstractedly, gazing after the turnout, and wondering how this proud and reticent man would like for his daughter to marry a penniless and obscure preacher.

The change in his tone which showed his thoughts to be with the rich man and not upon himself, Badgett, stirred the usually good-natured loafer to anger.

"I said," he repeated, raising his voice, "that folks that kin git their start by stealin' di'mon's kin efford to drive fine hosses, an' go to Congress, an' set at a table loden with gold, an' silver, an' champagne."

"What do you mean?" demanded Kennison, staring at him blankly.

"I mean what I say," replied Badgett, doggedly; "I mean that Van Herrin' yonder is a thief, an' a double thief, for he stole di'mon's from a dead woman. You ain't never heerd that tale, parson? Then ax the first man you run acrost; fer ever' man, woman an' chile in Thornham knows that Van Herrin' was ez poor ez I am, ontell the night he sneaked out'n Roseneath yander with Miss Elinor Thornham's di'mon's under his arm. An' I wish my Maker would strike me stone dead ef I did n't see him with my own eyes."

"You had better go home, Badgett," said Kennison, seizing him by the collar and looking sternly in his face. "You have been drinking."

"Drinkin'!" echoed Badgett, angrily, shaking himself loose. "Let go o' me, d—n you! You 're a plum out-'n'-out gentleman, parson," he added with sullen humility, "but you 're liable to mistakes. Ax the first man you run acrost about Van Herrin', an' Miss Elinor's di'mon's."

He walked away, leaving his antagonist rooted where he stood and speechless with anger.

Kennison's brain was in a whirl. What did it mean? Did it mean anything?

"Pshaw!" he ejaculated with a laugh, resuming his walk, "the envious froth of a foolish man's tongue!" But his exhilaration was gone. Strive as he would he could not recall that image of his bride in her white and virgin loveliness. Badgett's words returned with teasing insistence; and certain half-uttered phrases, heretofore meaningless, began to shape themselves, unconsciously, into clearness in his troubled brain.

"Ax the first man you run acrost;" he repeated Badgett's words monotonously. "I will not!" he replied to himself angrily. "I will," he finally exclaimed. "At least I will see what the idle report means."

He quickened his steps again until he reached the business portion of the street. Here he looked about him uncertainly; then perceiving a light in an upper room of one of the weather-beaten houses, he ran up the outer stair, that climbed shakily to the second floor, and tapped on the door. It was opened by Andrew Barclay of the firm of Barclay and Wright, an elderly man, a lawyer, and one of his own parishioners.

"Why, good-evening, Mr. Kennison," he

said cordially. "Come in, come in. I am glad to see you."

Kennison suddenly appeared ridiculous in his own eyes.

"I only stopped," he stammered, "to speak to you about the matter of repairs at the church — I beg your pardon, Mr. Barclay," he continued with an abrupt change of manner, and a return to his usual quiet dignity, "I came for personal reasons. Will you allow me a few moments' talk?"

"Certainly," responded Mr. Barclay, closing the door and leading the way into his inner office, where he placed a chair for his visitor, and seated himself.

Again Kennison drew back. A quick sense of his own treachery to his friend and to his betrothed swept over him. But he steadied himself and leaned forward.

"Mr. Barclay," he began, "I have to-day for the first time heard a very serious charge — a charge of theft — brought against one of my friends and parishioners. The source from which this information reached me is a very doubtful one. But I feel justified in investigating its truth. I refer to the report that Colonel Herring — For reasons personal to myself, I desire to hear the story

— which I am confident is false, or grossly exaggerated — from some responsible person. Will you give me the facts in the case?"

Mr. Barclay got up from his chair, sat down again, and coughed aimlessly once or twice.

"Really, Mr. Kennison," he said, "I hardly know how to reply. There was certainly a curious robbery here in Thornham some twelve or thirteen years ago; and circumstances at the time seemed to implicate Van — Colonel Herring. But "—

"You will oblige me by relating the affair just as it happened," interrupted Kennison in a tone of authority.

Andrew Barclay was a conscientious man; he prided himself on his straightforwardness, and on the entire absence of prejudice in his profession. But his profession had also cultivated a certain dramatic talent which he possessed; and although he began Vanborough Herring's story with the intention of giving simply an unbiased statement, yet as he proceeded, his own secret conviction that there was something rotten at the core of the successful man's life tinged his words. He related the details of Elinor Thornham's death as if he had been present;

almost unconsciously he added as facts the later exaggerations that had crept into the story; his sonorous voice rose and fell with cadenced emphasis; he felt himself thrilled with his own eloquence as he described the tragic death of Young Van, and the sudden snatching away of the wife and two children.

"The Hand of God sometimes delays," he concluded, "but it is heavy when it does strike."

His auditor, who had sat motionless through the long recital, rose as if jerked upward by a spring.

"I am very much obliged to you, Mr. Barclay," he said in a heavy monotonous voice. "One question, if you please. Why was Colonel Herring never prosecuted?"

"Oh," returned the lawyer with a shrug of his shoulders, "family pride. The Thornhams themselves would have been disgraced if a kinsman of their own had gone to the penitentiary."

"Thank you, Mr. Barclay," Kennison said again; "good-evening."

Barclay listened with a bewildered air to the echo of his retreating footsteps on the stair outside. Suddenly he dashed his hand to his forehead with a groan.

"Oh, Lord, what have I done!" he cried. "What an old ass I am. I had forgotten! They say he is to marry Olive Herring. Poor little Olive! Kennison!" he shouted, springing precipitately to the door; "Mr. Kennison!" he called again, possessed by a wild desire to take it all back, somehow. But the stairway, which was now quite dark, was empty.

.   .   .   .

The young preacher entered his study, hardly knowing how he got there, and lighted his student-lamp. His nearly finished sermon lay on the table; he glanced at it indifferently, and at the loose sheet beside it, upon which he had that morning written some verses dedicated to Olive Herring. He picked up the latter and mechanically corrected an error; then dropping it, he began to walk restlessly up and down the small room.

"A common thief!" he ejaculated, flushing and paling by turns. "No, not a common thief, by heaven! A rich, successful, ambitious thief. . . . It is incredible, I will not believe it! . . . And yet, is there room for doubt? Barclay certainly believes him guilty. . . . *Olive*, the daughter of a man publicly branded as a coward and a criminal! It cannot, cannot be! . . . But . . . dare I, have I the right to marry a woman upon whose family rests even such a suspicion? Do I not owe something to my calling? . . . A taint in the blood of *my wife!* . . . A stain upon *my wife's* name! . . . O Olive! . . . Olive! . . . *My God!*" he groaned aloud, and falling upon his knees he strove to pray; but the words which rose to his lips had no meaning.

The night wore away in a conflict between what he believed to be love and duty. When he appeared before his congregation the next morning, his extreme pallor startled those nearest him. To Olive, who stole a glance at him as he entered, this was but the visible trace of the same emotion which had kept her awake the livelong night; and her heart throbbed with secret exultation. No one else suspected its cause; for neither June Badgett nor Andrew Barclay was present.

The voice with which Kennison began his sermon was weak and husky. He had no notes before him, for it was not the sermon which he had nearly finished the day before, and which still lay, untouched, on the study-table. He chose for his text the words:

"*But God is faithful, who will not suffer
you to be tempted above that ye are able.*"
His theme was self-sacrifice. Moved by the
hidden springs of wretchedness and indeci-
sion within him, he spoke with a fervor
which stirred his listeners to enthusiasm; his
voice gathered strength as he proceeded, and
his pale face shone as with the glory of
martyrdom.

Olive Herring, in her pew, with Madame
de Jolibois seated beside her, heard the voice
of the speaker as through a dream; the
sense of his words penetrated but vaguely to
her understanding. Her feeling for the man
overpowered for the moment all thought of
the preacher and his vocation. She dared
not glance at him lest the conscious look in
her eyes should disturb his impassioned flow
of thought. She might indeed have gazed
her fill, for he kept his own eyes sedulously
turned away from that part of the church in
which she sat.

" The parson wrastled like he had a powerful purchase on ole Satan!" remarked
Dud Welsh with a laugh to his companion,
as they walked away from the church together.

"Poor young man!" commented Miss

Kizzy to Olive. "He must have some hidden trouble, a thorn in the flesh, like St. Paul."

Olive did not reply, but she smiled, secure in the knowledge of their secret, his and hers!

She waited for him through the drowsy afternoon in the shady summer-house, disappointed but no-wise disturbed by his non-appearance.

"Sunday is always a busy day with him; he will come to-morrow," she whispered to herself confidently, answering the summons to dinner.

Herring looked up at his daughter as she entered the dining-room, and glanced at the vacant places usually occupied by Jeffrey and Kennison. He moved uneasily in his chair and seemed about to question her, but checked himself, evidently reassured by her calm and happy face.

"What a delightful dinner-party!" he said gayly as they arose from the table. "Better company than all the senators and judges, planters and preachers we have been accustomed to dine with lately, eh, Olive?"

He drew her hand through his arm and walked with her up and down the long gal-

lery, chatting almost eagerly. It was the first
time his daughter ever remembered to have
seen him like this — though those who had
known him in former times would have exclaimed, "The old Van Herring!" He was
boyishly enthusiastic, talking of his plans for
himself and her; and overflowing with what
seemed to her a new-born tenderness. It
was an evening long to be remembered.

She wished to speak to him of Kennison,
but refrained — for her lover had begged to
be allowed to plead his own cause. But she
had no longer any doubts. She felt that
he divined her happiness and rejoiced in it.

"Oh! how noble he is, my father! my
hero!" she murmured when with his good-
night kiss on her brow, she went up to her
own room. "No wonder that he and Mark"
— she breathed the name shyly — "no wonder they were drawn to each other from the
first."

Nor had the father's unwonted mood
passed the next morning. He laughed and
jested with his daughter over the breakfast-
table, and lingered talking to her long after
his usual hour for leaving the house. When
at length he kissed her and drove away in
the direction of Fair View, he looked back

to shout a greeting to her. She waved her hand, standing on the high steps, but gave a sudden start, as a vague picture floated suddenly through her brain — a picture of Young Van riding away to his death that spring morning! The vision passed as quickly as it came, and she ran down into the rose-garden.

She was in the little morning-room when Kennison came. The half-withered flowers which he had gathered for her the Saturday before were in a vase on the table beside her. She sprang to meet him with a glad smile. He came forward slowly, and barely touched her outstretched hands with his, which were cold and clammy.

"Olive," he began, "Miss Herring" — he paused, confused by the growing wonder in her eyes; "I — I" — he went on desperately, — " since I saw you last, I have heard the story of Miss Thornham's diamonds " —

" Miss Thornham's diamonds ? " repeated Olive, puzzled.

" And — and of your — of Colonel Herring's supposed connection with their disappearance," he stammered.

"Of my father's " —

He interrupted her eagerly. He was no

longer conscious of what he said, but seemed possessed by a mad haste to unburden himself of the terrible story; the words poured from his lips in an irresistible torrent. To do him justice, it had not occurred to him that the daughter might, by some miracle, through all these years, have been spared the knowledge of her father's dishonor. He told the story, not indeed as it had been told him; sparing her instinctively, softening ugly phrases and suppressing many details. But he told it, nevertheless.

When he left his study after a second sleepless and wretched night, he had not known definitely what he meant to say to her. Certainly he had not foreseen that the sight of her would arouse in him an insane desire to justify to his own better nature the course he had decided upon pursuing. What he had called duty seemed to him, as he concluded, the basest cowardice.

She heard him to the end, standing motionless before him, with her arms hanging, and her eyes fixed upon his face.

"Do you really mean to tell me, Mr. Kennison," she said slowly when he had finished, "that the people of Thornham, my father's friends and neighbors, who have known him since his early manhood, have for thirteen years believed him to be an unscrupulous criminal? And that, believing him to be so base, they have continued to associate with him and his family? to come to his house and accept his hospitality?"

Kennison did not reply. A terrible conviction was forcing itself upon him.

"Can it be, Olive," he panted, horror-stricken, "that you have never heard this story before?"

"I have never heard it," she returned in a hard voice, "and I wish you to understand, Mr. Kennison, that I know it to be false — wickedly, monstrously, cruelly false. My father," she lifted her head proudly, — "my father! the truest, bravest, gentlest, and most loyal gentleman — *my father!*" she put her hand to her throat to check a rising sob there.

Kennison, overwhelmed by a sense of his own brutality, fairly staggered, clutching at a corner of the table for support. "My God, what have I done! O, Olive, can you ever forgive" —

"Will you be good enough to go," she interrupted coldly. Then, suddenly losing control of herself, she cried passionately,

"Go! can you not see that your presence is an insult to my father's daughter!"

He made no further appeal, but stood looking at her in silence, devouring every detail of her lovely face, scorching under the fire of her beautiful angry eyes.

"You cannot despise me more than I despise myself," he said at length. With these words he quitted the room and the house.

Her courage sustained her until the echo of his footsteps died away. Then, with a shuddering cry, she dropped to the floor and buried her face in her hands. A world of unheeded half-forgotten things rushed upon her, — significant glances, whispered phrases, a hint here, a shake of the head there; the words spoken by Young Van when he lay a-dying . . . had she really heard them then? they rang loudly enough in her ears now! . . . the strange and unaccountable change in her father's manner. Oh, she remembered now how joyous and gay he used to be at the " other house," and how constrained and silent after —

"Oh, my mother, my poor mother, and poor, poor little Van!" she moaned. "And I alone, through all these wretched years, have been foolishly, heartlessly, blindly gay and light-hearted. Why have they not told me! Oh, the vile, horrible lie! *Father! Father!*"

Through her grief and rage there came now and then another and a keener pang. But this she resolutely put aside.

"He never loved me," she said sternly, "or instead of giving me up, he would surely have gathered me in his arms and sheltered me from all pain. That would have been my father's way — or Duncan's. Does Duncan know, I wonder? Oh, I cannot, cannot bear it."

The recurring thought was intolerable, and, stung beyond endurance, she sought her old nurse, and, laying her head against her bosom, she found relief in a paroxysm of tears.

"Somep'n 's wrong wi' de chile," mused Betty, stroking the soft hair. "An' de preacher-man is sho at de bottom of it!" But neither then nor later did she suspect the whole truth.

Soothed into at least a semblance of quiet, Olive awaited with feverish impatience her father's return. She would throw herself into his arms and tell it all to him, — her remorse at not having guessed that some trouble had clouded his, her mother's, Young Van's lives; her shame at having been so frivolous, — all, all!

She ran to meet him in the late afternoon. He saw her on the steps as he turned in at the park-gateway, and shouted a greeting as he had done that morning. But his face changed when he looked closely into hers. She did throw herself into his arms, but the words she wished to utter died in her throat. There rose up on the instant between the father and daughter the impenetrable barrier which for so many years had lain impassable between the husband and wife.

He kissed her tenderly, asked a few commonplace questions concerning the day's occupations, and passed into his library, closing the door behind him. Then followed for Vanborough Herring perhaps the bitterest hour of his life. He had read but too clearly in the wistful eyes.

He knew that she knew!

X

ELINOR THORNHAM.

WHEN it became known in Thornham that the visits both of Kennison and Jeffrey to Roseneath had ceased abruptly, there was an outburst of curiosity. And, as usual, there were not wanting theories to explain the fact; some asserted that Miss Herring had dismissed both men in favor of a third — unknown — admirer; others declared that Herring had peremptorily forbidden them both his house; one rumor had it that Jeffrey, the fortunate man, was ostentatiously absenting himself in order to throw gossip off the scent; another gravely demonstrated that neither suitor had been really in earnest, and the pursuit had been discontinued by a mutual understanding between them, leaving the field free to whoever chose to enter it. A few had an inkling of the truth. Among these was Andrew Barclay, who, uneasy and contrite, at length sought his pastor, and quite humbly confessed that, carried away by professional enthusiasm, he had exaggerated the story of the theft.

"The bottom facts, as known, would not convict," he concluded remorsefully.

"Pray think no more about the matter, Mr. Barclay," the preacher returned. "If I have made mistakes in this affair I alone am to blame." He spoke with a certain dull weariness. Something had gone out of the man. From that time forward, truly, there was no talk of changes and reforms in St. John's Church. The rector's sermons were quite orthodox, and singularly colorless. Then, by a contradiction not unusual in human nature, those who had cried out most loudly against his innovations and his latitude of creed, cried out more loudly still against his want of progress.

.   .   .   .

The young mistress of Roseneath found the days which followed Kennison's revelation well-nigh unbearable; she shrank painfully from contact with the people of the village; she would gladly have denied herself even to Rose, in whose subtly changed face she read a knowledge of the shameful story. Wrung with sympathy for her father, to whom she felt immeasurably nearer, yet from whom in some inexplicable way, too, she was infinitely removed, she proudly forbore to question even her old nurse. Thus, turned upon herself and tortured by uncertainty and self-pity, it seemed for a time as if she were about to succumb like her mother before her; her step became listless, her eyes lost their sparkle. Her father watched her with a solicitude doubled by the recollection of his former losses. But something of his own indomitable spirit presently arose within her, and she found herself able to smile calmly into familiar faces, while intuitively selecting from those about her the few who had known how, unquestioning, to trust a friend.

Nevertheless the change in her outward appearance was great; a reserve which bordered upon hauteur took the place of her girlish frankness; her open straightforward gaze became cool and searching; her movements were less quick and impulsive. The stately dignity of her bearing enhanced her beauty a thousand fold.

This sudden transformation seemed little less than marvelous to those unacquainted with its secret spring.

In a short time, fearful of disappointing

or injuring her father, she resumed as nearly as possible the life which had been so rudely interrupted, filling Roseneath — beautiful under the blue autumnal skies — with guests and giving it a semblance at least of all its former gayety. Kennison she saw only from a distance, or from the pew in his church, which she continued to occupy, bearing the keen gaze of the public with such proud calm that criticism was disarmed and gossip itself disconcerted.

Jeffrey had resumed somewhat of his old position in the household, though his visits were fewer and of a more formal character.

He sat with her one day, watching her active preparations for the coming season in Washington — for Herring, as had been foreseen, had received an almost unanimous vote at the election. "Olive," he said resolutely, though with an embarrassed air, "Kennison has ceased to come to Roseneath. Does that mean " —

"I am no longer engaged to Mr. Kennison," she interrupted, a trifle haughtily.

His face brightened. He arose and made a movement toward her. "Then . . . you have read your own heart more truly . . . you have found that you do not love him.

. . . Perhaps? . . . Olive, will you . . . is it too soon for me to speak again? . . . Will you be my wife?"

She shrank from him with a gesture of horror.

"Oh, no!" she cried, "no, that is for-ever impossible!"

"Olive," said her father, entering at that moment with an open letter in his hand, "we shall have to leave sooner than I had thought. To-morrow, if possible. Betty will accompany us. Liberty will remain behind to close the house, and follow later. Duncan, my boy," he laid his hand with unwonted familiarity on the young man's shoulder, "Thornham is a dull place for a man with a soul; come with us to Washing-ton."

Jeffrey glanced at Olive before he replied. "Thank you, Colonel," he said warmly, "I wish I could; but the grinding at Good Luck is in full blast and I must be here to look after it."

He crossed the river the next morning to the station to see them off. A large num-ber of Colonel Herring's constituents were gathered about him on the platform; and several of Olive's friends, including Madame de Jolibois and Rose, had followed her into the car. Rose clung, weeping, to her friend, but she smiled through her tears. "The things you sent came this morning, Olive," she whispered; "the cabin will be lovely when they are all in place. And I know I will like keeping house for my father."

"I am sure you will, dear," returned Olive, kissing the small upturned face.

"If you should meet Monshur *dee* Jolly-boys in the sumptuous Halls of our Nation's Metropolis" — began Miss Kizzy, but the train which had been making threatening movements for half an hour was at last really about to start, and Jeffrey hurried her away, cutting short her studied apostrophe.

.   .   .   .

The Honorable Vanborough Herring and his daughter entered at once into the social life of the Capital. The great wealth and distinguished air of the one, and the beauty and charm of the other, made them a welcome addition even to that wide and brilliant circle.

To the girl, who saw her father for the first time unconstrained and wholly at ease, the transition from the pain and wretchedness of the past weeks to sudden joyous com-

panionship with him was like a birth into
some new world; the hideous dream was remembered only when some chance word or
inadvertent reference brought into his eyes
the look which said, " Thus far shalt thou
come — even thou — and no farther."

The outer life of the great city interested
and amused her. Balls, dinners, the theatre,
— routs of all kinds, following each other in
endless succession, found the young stranger
always the centre of a host of admirers. If
a word or look from any of these brought to
her a memory of a twilight hour in the old
summer-house at Roseneath, and of a pair of
dark eyes glowing with masterful love, there
was at least nothing in her own to betray
the thought.

One night toward the end of February
she came down the stairway of their handsome apartment dressed for a ball, given
in honor of a foreign embassy. Her shoulders arose white and gleaming above the
foamy lace of her satin gown; jewels
flashed on her bare arms and shone in her
hair. Beautiful and imperious, her face
showed no trace of the shock which, but a
few months earlier, had stunned her into
apathy. Midway on the stair she paused

and threw up her head, like a deer in the
forest, which scents a presence on the morning air. Betty, following her with a heap
of furred wraps on her arm, stopped also
and chuckled softly.

"I knows dat voice, too, Miss Olive! You
ain' mistakened, chile. It's Mars Duncan."

It was Duncan who stood talking gayly
with her father in the drawing-room, and
looking very bright and handsome. He
came forward to meet her.

"I have this moment arrived," he said,
when the warm unembarrassed greetings were
over, "and as I am leaving to-morrow" —

"To-morrow!" echoed his hosts in a
breath.

"Yes," he explained, "I have leased
Good Luck for a couple of years (the crop,
by the way, this year, Colonel, was the
heaviest ever handled on the plantation) to
Lester, with the privilege of renewing or
buying me out at the end of that time. My
other business is in such a. shape that it
does not require my personal attention. I
am going to knock around Europe for a
year or two, — perhaps longer, — and I am
hurrying to join some old college friends in
New York who sail on Saturday."

Colonel Herring rang for Liberty and ordered his carriage to be dismissed.

"We will spend the evening at home, Olive?" he said, half-questioningly.

"Oh, yes," she acquiesced quickly.

Jeffrey protested but faintly, his gaze wandering hungrily over her as she sat near him with the firelight playing over her shimmering gown; her head resting on her hand, and her luminous eyes fixed upon his face.

The evening sped but too quickly. He sighed involuntarily as he rose to go.

"Wait a moment, Duncan," said Herring, "I wish to give you a couple of letters to some friends in London." He walked into the library, and Olive and Duncan, left alone, relapsed into a silence through which they could hear the scratching of the pen on paper through the draped doorway.

"Olive," the young man said at last in a low tone, "I have been hoping that you would ask me to stay, or that you would come with me. Am I foolish to speak again? Yet I must. Will you not give yourself to me, Olive?"

"No, Duncan," she replied as before, "that is quite impossible." But seeing him turn away, the tears sprang to her eyes.

She laid her hand on his arm beseechingly. " But — but you will not forget me, Duncan, — your childhood's friend, your sister ? You will write us sometimes ; you will think of us — of me ? "

" Forget you ! " he exclaimed, taking her hands in his warm clasp. " Olive, do you imagine that I will not go on loving you as long as I live ! Do you think, dear, that I could put you out of my life if I tried ! " He paused and added, smiling a little, " It runs in my family to be faithful. My uncle — perhaps you never knew that, Olive ? — my uncle died, an old man, — true to the one woman he had ever loved and whom he lost in his early manhood. Oh yes. I will write," he continued, as Herring reëntered the room with the letters in his hand, " and perhaps one day " —

He left the significant sentence, uttered in her father's presence, unfinished, and departed.

" Duncan is a fine fellow ; I wish you could have loved him well enough to marry him, Olive," Herring said, after a long silence, during which he mused with his eyes fixed abstractedly on the fire.

These were the only words he ever uttered which betrayed his knowledge of what had been passing in his daughter's life.

"I cannot marry Duncan," she replied, paling. "I shall never marry. Why should I?" she continued in a lighter tone, coming over and putting her arms about his neck, "have I not you?"

.   .   .   .

Herring's private affairs in the late spring necessitated a flying trip to Thornham; he announced this to Olive, suggesting, though but half-heartedly, that she remain in Washington during his brief absence.

"How dare you hint such a thing!" she cried with saucy indignation. "No, indeed! You are too attractive by far to be allowed to travel alone, Colonel Herring! Even in stupid old Thornham some woman might set a trap for you"—

"Miss Kizzy?" he demanded demurely.

"Now, papa," she admonished gravely, with uplifted finger. "You know that Monshur *dee* Jollyboys is a husband. And there would certainly be bloodshed!"

Whereat they laughed like a pair of children.

Liberty, who had preceded them, met them on their arrival at Thornham.

"De river's on a big rise, Mars Van," he remarked, leading the way to the carriage.

The horses threw up their heads, and pulled back with quivering nostrils and trembling flanks, when he attempted to lead them on the ferry-boat which rose and fell on the swirling current, and it was some moments before he succeeded in calming them.

The steadily rising water, blood-red and flecked with foam, was within a foot of the grass-grown edge of the high bluffs. Its surface was covered with floating débris, — tree-trunks, broken barrels, hencoops, bits of shingle, what not, from above, which made it difficult for John Hopson, the old ferryman, to manage the passage. Jack Addington, standing in the door of his warehouse, which seemed dangerously near the bank, saw them approaching and came out to greet them. He was a small, shrewd-looking man, with a forceful face and pleasant quizzical eyes.

"I think we are in for a whizzer this time, Colonel," he said. "I hope Fair View is in good shape to stand it?"

"Oh yes," responded Herring confidently, "but how about the warehouse?"

"Well," said Addington, "I'm trusting

some in Providence, and a good deal in bricks and mortar, for the warehouse. You look like a Roseneath rose, Olive! Making laws for your country agrees with you."

He removed his foot from the carriage-step and they drove rapidly to Roseneath, where, five minutes later, Betty was scolding Big Hannah, and browbeating 'Liza and Job, for all manner of (presumable) crimes committed during her absence.

It was very peaceful and quiet at the old place. Olive came out upon the gallery about an hour before sunset, and stood looking over the familiar landscape. The magnolias shading the steps were starred with great white cups; the wholesome odor of these mingled with the perfume of damask-roses — " Mother-roses," she and Van used to call them! — abloom in the rose-garden. A boat was slipping Gulf-ward on the river, its black hull dancing high on the swollen stream; a light wind swayed the tops of the live-oaks. She turned her eyes in the direction of the village, where the slim needle of St. John's spire arose above the surrounding roofs; a slight flush colored her cheeks, and an inscrutable smile played about her lips.

" Papa ! " she called to Herring, who sat

at his library-table within, writing. "Do not work any longer to-day. Come on the gallery with me."

He rose obediently, gathering some papers together and thrusting them into his breast-pocket, and came out. He passed his hand wearily over his forehead ; he looked care-worn and pale.

"Why, father," she cried, " are you ill ? "

He shook his head, smiling.

" Then you are very tired, and no wonder ; sit here and rest."

She pulled a chair forward, and when he was seated she nestled on the floor at his feet, leaning her head against his knee.

He stroked her hair absently with his hand.

"Olive," he asked abruptly, after a moment's silence, "do you remember your cousin, Elinor Thornham ? "

The question drove the blood from her heart ; her lips trembled so that she could not speak. But the quiet look on his face as she glanced furtively up reassured her.

" Why yes," she said, " I remember her. She sent for me once — here. I can dimly recall her face bending over me while she held me on her lap. She gave me a doll which had been hers when she was a child.

I think, though I am not quite sure, that Big Hannah and I broke it the same day! Afterward, one day when Van and I were playing in the garden at the other house, she called us to her carriage in passing, and talked to us. Oh yes, I remember her."

"You are like her, Olive, wonderfully like her. She was very beautiful," he mused more to himself than to his daughter. Then, slowly and formally as if rehearsing a carefully thought-out tale, he went on: "I was hardly more than a lad when I came to Thornham, Olive, — fresh from college, and poor, but full of energy and ambition. The Thornhams and the Vanboroughs — my mother's people — were closely related; and it was at the suggestion of Steven Thornham — her father — that I left Kentucky to try my fortune in Texas. She was but a slip of a girl when I first saw her — here at Roseneath. She had no sisters; and John, her only brother, had left home, after a bitter quarrel with his father, four or five years before. The mother's heart was with her exiled boy; the father was stormy and eccentric; but in spite of this, Roseneath was very gay; and Elinor, as young as she was, was the acknowledged leader of the social life — then very brilliant — in Thornham. She was very beautiful, high-spirited, and somewhat willful, and the idol of her father, who somehow favored my suit from the first; for, from the moment I came into her presence, I began to love Elinor Thornham."

Olive made an involuntary movement, shrinking almost imperceptibly away from him; but he drew her head again to his knee and continued : —

"Among her many suitors I had but one rival, Peter Newall. Perhaps you cannot think of him, Olive, as an ardent wooer, — shabby quiet old Newall! But in those days he also was young and eager, with life before him. And he loved her; he had loved her long before I ever saw her, — since she was a little girl; and I think — I know — that she was fond of him. But it was I whom she loved! It had all come about so naturally that the possibility of any change or interruption to the course of our love-life never troubled me. Her father stipulated only that we should wait until my law-practice should be on a firmer basis. It was the rosy morning of my life."

His voice lost its monotony and thrilled with exultant passion.

" I saw her daily. There is not a path in the rose-garden yonder that I have not walked with her, nor a nook or corner about Roseneath in which some memory of that happy time does not linger. The date was fixed for our marriage, when her father died suddenly; and in less than two months Mrs. Thornham followed him, leaving Elinor alone in the world, except for the almost unknown brother who lived in New Orleans, and who was abroad at the time of his mother's death. Up to this moment Elinor's affection for me had seemed boundless. Through the trying time of her mother's death and burial she clung to me as her only and natural protector, and we had arranged that the marriage, in spite of her mourning, should take place at once. No man, surely, was ever happier than I was the morning a summons came from my betrothed bride appointing an hour for me to call at Roseneath. Strange as this summons seemed, since I was in the habit of spending a part of every day at Roseneath, I yet had no suspicion of anything wrong. At the appointed hour I found her in the summer-house waiting for me. She seemed utterly transformed. Her manner was cold to haughtiness, her voice was hard, her lips set and cruel. I gazed at her in dismay while she told me in a few measured words that our engagement was at an end. She declined giving her reasons; but when I stormed and raved against her cruelty, she admitted that she had ceased to love me. I pleaded in vain; she begged my forgiveness indeed when she saw my despair. When I thought it over afterward, I seemed to remember a softening light in her eyes, and a quivering about the corners of her mouth; but at the time I was half-blind with anger and mortification, and I saw nothing. I flung myself away from her with words which I do not now like to recall. The next day I left Thornham for my old home in Kentucky, persuaded I would never return.

"There I met again the little girl, grown to womanhood since I had last seen her, to whom in our school-days I had plighted my boyish troth, — Jeanie, your mother, Olive, the sweetest, truest, most loyal woman and wife that ever blessed a man's heart and home!"

He lifted his hand, wet with Olive's tears, to his own brimming eyes. The child's heart throbbed with exquisite emotion at this tribute to the mother for whose memory a moment before she had felt such jealous pangs.

Herring remained silent a short time. When he resumed there was a change in his tone, as if some mighty undercurrent of feeling, to which the history of his love-life had been but a prelude, were about to make itself felt.

"We were both poor — Jeanie and I — though some of my family were rich and influential; and after a time we decided to come to Thornham, where I owned a small piece of property — the 'other house,' which Van and his mother loved so. She knew the story of my early love, but she had no fear, for she also knew that Elinor Thornham was less than the shadow of a shade in my life, beside her own blooming image. We were very happy in the cottage where you were all born, Olive, though I was still poor, and Jeanie had to make many sacrifices. I saw Elinor occasionally. She was a semi-invalid and lived alone in this lonely house with her housekeeper and her servants. She called on my wife when we first came to Thornham; and we made one or two visits to Roseneath. But her health soon failed entirely, and she ceased to go anywhere. Yes, we were very happy. No wonder my boy longed for that 'other house!'

"Well . . . the years passed. . . . One morning, Liberty, who was Elinor's butler, brought a note to my office. It was a summons — for the second time — to Roseneath. The hour fixed was half past eight o'clock the same evening. I confess that my heart stirred a little when I saw the handwriting, but the feeling uppermost was curiosity. As night approached, I found myself growing impatient, and as soon as the hour struck, I left home and walked out the familiar road to Roseneath. The moon was shining brightly as I passed along the avenue to the house; but I saw no one, and when I reached the door it was opened for me by Elinor herself; so pale, so weak and trembling, that she fell almost fainting in my arms. I carried her into the sitting-room and laid her upon the couch. When she recovered sufficiently to speak, she explained that she had purposely sent every one out of the way, wishing to see me alone and without question or comment, even from her own family."

Olive was listening now with a strained attention that caused her heart to stand still.

"She was thin and worn, but she was still beautiful, as she lay there lifting her large lustrous eyes to mine."

"*Something in a man dies hard!*" Olive seemed to hear the echo of old Isham's words in her father's voice.

"I need not tell you all that passed between us; though the interview was not a long one. She felt that death was upon her; and she wished before she died to tell me why she had broken the sacred vows that had once bound our lives together. I can see her now, — her slight form supported by pillows, clad in the soft and clinging white she loved! She held in her hand a small jewel-box, — the cursed necklet, which, as sure as there is a God in Heaven, caused the death of my wife, and of my son."

The last words broke from him in a sort of fury. But he seemed unconscious of having uttered them. His daughter's heart throbbed painfully. Kennison's story rushed back upon her. What was she about to hear? She could hardly forbear crying out and beseeching him, in mercy to himself and to her, to say no more!

But he took up the thread again.

"This is what she told me, stopping often to take breath, for she was pitifully weak and suffering. I knelt, helpless, beside the couch. She had never ceased to love me. Her whole heart, from the moment she saw me first, was mine, and mine only. But — a malady which had kept her delicate, as a child, and troubled her girlhood — curious lapses of consciousness, which left her faint and ill — it was only after her mother's death, and when she was doubly orphaned, that she knew its nature and meaning — *Epilepsy.* She had been kept in ignorance of the very word. Almost by chance she had heard it applied to the attack which seized her a few days after her mother's death. She insisted upon knowing from the physician who had attended her from her babyhood the nature of the disease; and horror-stricken at his explanation, she determined not to commit the crime of marriage. But she could not bring herself to tell me the real reason. Perhaps she feared her own power of resistance; for she must have known that such an argument would have small weight in a lover's eyes. And she chose rather to let me believe her false and cruel. You know already how the engagement ended. . . . When I left her, I opened a window and went out upon the gallery, and crossed the rose-garden."

He stopped and leaned back in his large chair. Olive — all her senses wrought to agony — was listening still.

" And — and the necklet, father, the diamonds?" she said, unable longer to endure the suspense.

" Oh, the cursed diamonds!" his voice was thick and smothered; he spoke as if his tongue were cleaving to the roof of his mouth. " Yes, the diamonds. I took them from her, and put " —

Again he was silent; so long that the silence became intolerable. She pressed closer to him, trembling in every limb.

" Yes, father, I know how it was," she stammered eagerly. " I understand perfectly. You need not mind telling me. I know that you meant to give them back . . . the next day. Oh, father, you *did* mean to give them back?"

A heavy groan was the only response. She felt a sort of shiver pass through the hand she held in hers.

XI.

DEATH IN LIFE.

OLIVE sprang to her feet, startled by a nameless fear. Her father's head had fallen to one side; his eyes were partly closed and devoid of expression; his lips were rigid; one arm hung inert at his side; the other, as Olive loosened her hold upon it, fell like a lifeless thing across his breast.

The girl's terrified shrieks aroused the household; the servants flocked in.

"Don't be skeered, Miss Olive," Liberty said confidently, "'t ain't nothin' but a faintin'-fit."

He lifted his master in his strong arms, and bore him into an inner room, where they exhausted, without apparent effect, the usual remedies. It seemed a long time to the helpless watchers before the doctor came; it was in reality but a short half-hour.

He was accompanied by Newall, who chanced to be at his office when the messenger arrived. He cleared the room of all but Liberty, and began a close examination of his patient. It was some time before he came out upon the gallery, where Olive, pale and agitated, awaited him, in company with the lawyer.

"Is he better, Doctor Alsbury?" she demanded eagerly. "Has he revived?"

"He is sleeping," the doctor answered evasively; "send some one to town with this prescription at once," he added, handing her a slip of paper.

"Is it death?" asked Newall, when she was out of hearing.

The doctor shook his head.

"It is worse than death," he said. "It is almost complete paralysis of the body, involving the brain."

"He cannot recover?"

"He cannot recover, except by a miracle; and he may live for years in this condition."

"My God!" groaned the lawyer; "who will tell his daughter this?"

"I will tell her myself," Doctor Alsbury said gravely; "or I will at least tell her what she must of necessity know: that her father has had a stroke of paralysis which will render him for some time absolutely helpless."

He did tell her, taking her apart, and remaining with her — less the physician than the lifelong friend of her father and mother — until the first paroxysm of agony had a little spent itself. Then at her own request he led her into the room where her father was.

The lamplight fell upon his face, for it was long past nightfall; his eyes stared vacantly from beneath their half-closed lids; he breathed heavily.

"He is awake," said the doctor, laying his palm gently upon the broad forehead.

The only perceptible difference between the sleeping and the waking state of the stricken man was in the slight lifting of the heavy eyelids, and a restless movement of the lips.

"It may be a long time before he will be able to move, Olive," Doctor Alsbury went on, looking down compassionately at the lifeless body and ghastly face. "He will have to be fed and cared for like an infant. Liberty will attend to that."

Liberty nodded, unable to speak; his massive chest was heaving and his dark cheeks were wet with tears.

The daughter had dropped with a wail of

anguish on her knees by the bedside, and was covering her father's motionless hand with kisses.

The next morning she followed the physician out of the room. She had watched through the long hours of the night with Liberty, — hoping, despairing, praying. It seemed monstrous that the returning light should have brought no change for the better.

" He is just the same? " she implored piteously.

" Yes, my child." The old doctor drew her head against his shoulder, striving to soothe her. " He is just the same. You must try and bear it."

She broke away from him and lifted her eyes earnestly to his face.

" Doctor Alsbury," she asked, " do you think my father is conscious? Do you think he can hear, or understand ? "

The doctor hesitated.

" I cannot tell," he replied slowly, " it may be, — it may possibly be."

She left him and walked swiftly back into her father's room.

" Please leave me alone with him a moment," she said gently to Madame de Jolibois and Mrs. Alsbury, who sat by the bed.

They went out softly, closing the door behind them.

She knelt beside him and laid her cheek against his; then, drawing back, she gazed steadily upon his face.

"He is awake," she sobbed tenderly, for the eyelids were partially raised. "Father," she said in a clear loud voice, "I am sure that you can hear your little girl. Listen, father, I love you. *I love you!* And I know that you did not carry away Elinor Thornham's jewels. My brave, true-hearted, hero-father! *I know that you did not take Elinor Thornham's diamonds.*"

There was not a quiver on the marble-like face; not a movement of the thick eyelashes. But she rose from her knees comforted. And from that day forward, as long as her father lived, her first act upon rising in the morning was to repeat, kneeling beside him, like a prayer, the same simple and fervent words.

.   .   .   .

The next day after Herring was stricken with paralysis, the river began to shrink once more within its banks. Jack Addington's warehouse stood, squat and sturdy, un-injured, with the marks of the flood on its rusty bricks; but this time the swirling waters did not spare Fair View; the young cane, wrenched up by the roots and trampled into the ground, was totally destroyed; fences, cabins, outhouses were beaten out of existence by the angry sweep of *The Arms of God;* the frightened live stock, huddled together in the fields, perished; the laborers, fleeing empty-handed, barely escaped with their lives. The destruction was complete!

XII.

ROSE.

"IT is inexplicable! It is incredible!"
the lawyer pushed the mass of papers before
him to one side of the table, and, leaning his
head on his hand, stared with frowning eyes
into space.

It was long past midnight; Peter Newall,
in his ill-lighted, shabby little office, had
been poring for hours over the documents
placed in his hands by Olive Herring, — letters, deeds, memoranda, receipts, accounts, —
everything pertaining to Vanborough Herring's business which she had been able to
find. They were methodically arranged,
labeled, and dated ; there was no confusion
or disarray about them. Herring had always attended to his own business affairs.
Only on rare occasions had he ever been
known to intrust any matter relating to his
private concerns into other hands. Newall's
investigation had therefore been easy enough.
The papers dated back to the purchase of

Roseneath, and included all transactions up to the moment of the late departure from Washington for Thornham. The revelation contained in these carefully annotated documents was of so extraordinary a nature that the lawyer, scarcely believing the evidence of his own senses, had returned to them again and again, but always with the same result.

The fabric which the successful advocate, politician, and planter had reared with such apparent ease, and which had reached such imposing proportions, was, it appeared, built upon a foundation so slender that it was already tottering to a fall under its own weight. Roseneath mortgaged to its full value; Fair View loaded with debt; notes falling due for which no provision could possibly be made; the very belongings of stables and outhouses unpaid for! There were indications showing that the master-hand which had planned and builded the structure had been at work, and the danger might for a time have been averted, or at least postponed. As it was, the ruin was inevitable and imminent.

"It is inconceivable," the lawyer repeated, "inexplicable. Poor, poor child!"

He arose and paced up and down the room, a thousand vague plans crowding upon his wearied brain; the only definite conclusion being a determination to keep from the daughter, so far as possible, the knowledge of her father's financial wreck, and her own helpless and dependent condition. In this, however, he reckoned without a sufficient understanding of the strong and resolute character of the girl herself.

" I wish to know exactly how my father's business affairs stand, Mr. Newall," she said quietly when that gentleman presented himself, a week later, at Roseneath, and began his carefully prepared statement.

" My dear child " — he stammered.

" Dear Mr. Newall," she interrupted, smiling a little at his discomfiture, "I saw enough in those papers before I put them into your hands to assure me, inexperienced as I am, that serious trouble was impending. I know that the crop at Fair View, upon which my father must have counted, is totally destroyed. I must know the exact truth. You need not be afraid of my strength or courage. I am my father's daughter."

It was now nearly a month since the fatal

stroke had fallen upon the master of Roseneath. The doctor's prognostication was but
too true. The inert body lay, day after day,
heavy, motionless, dead; always the same
vacant nearly closed eyes, the livid face, the
twitching lips, the muffled breathing. The
household, after the first days of terrified
expectation and despair, had fallen into a
forlorn sort of routine. Liberty and Betty
watched by turns at night; dressed and
undressed the nearly inanimate body, and
pressed, morsel by morsel, at proper intervals,
food and drink between the lips. Through
the long summer days Olive sat beside him,
slowly yielding up her hopes for his recovery. Miss Kizzy, Mrs. Alsbury, Newall,
Addington, and other friends came and went
from the silent chamber. Rose, with frightened face, hovered about the door, rarely
crossing the threshold. The idle servants
loitered about the great deserted rooms, gossiping in hushed whispers.

Olive looked at the lawyer in silence when
the papers had finally been examined, and all
legal technicalities clearly explained to her.

" It is worse than I thought," she said
at last. Her face was pale but determined.
" You will sell Fair View, of course," she

continued, "and arrange as far as possible
to have my father's debts paid"—

"My dear young lady," Newall hastened
to break in, "the homestead law of this State
allows you"—

"I am of age, or will be in a few weeks,"
she interrupted imperiously, "and I wish
everything sold that is salable. Every cent
must be applied to the payment of my father's debts. And we must of course leave
Roseneath at once."

Her lips quivered a little as she said this
and her eyes filled with tears.

"No, my child, no," replied Newall de-
cidedly. "I have a late letter from Mr.
B——, who holds the mortgage on Roseneath. He is not prepared to take control.
He desires for the sake of the place itself
that you should remain for the present in
the house."

This was perfectly true, though it was the
result of his own arguments and unbusiness-
like entreaties to the good-natured, wealthy
and careless young fellow who had advanced
a large sum of money to Herring on the
property.

"I am glad," she replied with a grateful
look. "It would be terrible for him to find

himself in a strange place when he recovers consciousness. But I must find something to do that will enable us to live "—

" Now, Olive," interrupted Newall eagerly, and with a hint of reproach in his voice, " you know that I have no one in the world but myself to look after, — selfish old bachelor that I am! I have known you since you were a baby; you are dearer to me than you dream of. I am not a rich man, but I have enough for us all. You are not too proud to let me take care of you and your father ? "

She clasped her hands about his arm and looked up in his face, struggling for a moment with the sobs in her throat.

" No, I am not too proud," she said at length. " I will be grateful, oh, more grateful than I can hope to tell you, for anything you can do for *him*. But I must help, dear friend. I must learn to support myself."

He went away, content perforce with this; and while busied with the by no means easy task of getting the most out of the ruined estate, arranging with creditors and selling off superfluous stock, he managed, with the help of Mrs. Alsbury and Madame de Jolibois, to get the promise of a few pupils for

his ward. In a little less than three months
from the day the envied young heiress
reached Thornham from Washington, Fair
View's new owner was rebuilding its fences;
the stables at Roseneath were empty; the
costlier furniture of the house was sold; the
servants, with the exception of Liberty and
Betty, were scattered far and wide; the
former master was lying helpless and unconscious in one of its rooms, while in another, a penniless girl was trying to earn
her daily living by teaching school.

.   .   .   .

The Hand of God, according to the open-
mouthed and awestruck gossips, had fallen
again — heavily, heavily!

.   .   .   .

It must not be supposed that Peter Newall was the only one of her father's old
friends who hastened with offers of practical
assistance to the forlorn young creature so
suddenly and so awfully bereft. More than
one of Herring's colleagues in office tried
— in ways more or less tactful — to place
her above the necessity of daily labor, —
the Alsburys; Major Burnham, fat, pursy,
and self-important, but kind-hearted; Jack
Addington, hesitating and embarrassed in

the depths of his stiff shirt-collar, and pretending that there was a balance — ahem — still unpaid on an old note — ahem — he 'd been owin' the Colonel for — ahem — he did n't know how many years; and above all, Miss Kizzy, who was ready to vacate her Doric-pillared mansion and dwell in the kitchen if only Vanborough — " Why, it was your father, Olive (poor as he was then), who took care of Serena while I, through Miss Thornham's generosity, studied the Saltatory Art in New Orleans, — though he would never let me tell it " — if only Olive and her father would take possession of it.

But all these offers, acknowledged with simple and unaffected gratitude, were declined, and the stuff of which she was made began to assert itself.

The young teacher chose for her school-room at Roseneath, not the remote upper hall where her own gay school-days had passed; but a spacious guest-chamber opening into the library and upon a curve of the wide gallery. From where she sat, with the row of small faces in front of her desk, she could see — in pleasant weather — her father, in the low wheeled chair which Liberty had constructed for him. Betty, after pushing him out into a vine-hung corner of the gallery, would sit beside him through the long mornings, sewing or mending, and crooning to herself and to him in a subdued voice familiar plantation lullabies. The school-children were so placed that they could not see him; Olive had contrived this, lest the sight of the swathed and motionless figure should frighten them.

It was but a handful of scholars which was intrusted at first — and most of them out of sheer pity — to the sometime chatelaine of Roseneath. Presently others came; for it was soon noised about the village that Miss Herring had a "knack" at teaching. She entered upon her new vocation timidly enough; but was surprised after a few days to find herself loving it for its own sake. Moreover, she loved the children and they loved her. As time passed on — for this was but the beginning of a succession of monotonous and uneventful days which stretched on into years — she regained, despite the death-in-life brooding over the house, much of her natural buoyancy; the color came back to her cheeks, the spring to her step.

They continued to live at Roseneath.

For, the mortgage foreclosed and the place offered for sale, no purchaser presenting himself, it remained, whether or no, in the hands of the mortgagee. The latter, after a visit to his property, wrote frankly to Newall. " I do not care to put any more money upon that elephant," he said. " If I see a chance to sell, I shall sell. If you can rent it to a good paying tenant, please do so. In the mean time, if Miss Herring will consent to remain in it and so keep it from dropping to pieces, I shall regard it as a favor to myself."

Thus, rarely going beyond the boundaries of the place, surrounded by innocently affectionate children, whom she taught after a happy fashion of her own, and seeing only the faces of the old and tried friends who came to her, she well-nigh forgot the shadow which had crushed her mother and brother, and darkened her father's career; that mysterious and terrible shadow which, falling upon herself, had in one swift moment changed her confidence into defiant mistrust, and chilled love itself out of her pathway. The unquestioning faith of her childhood, the innocent faith in God and man, — adorable in its simplicity, — had not returned to her ; nothing indeed can restore that, once it is lost! But her mind and heart, working silently over the problem of life, had found the higher faith which comes through earnest seeking. Of this the healthy inner and outer life — even in the midst of toil and anxiety — was the result. The time predicted for her had come : she had learned to feel and to think!

The Reverend Mark Kennison, in the early days of her father's affliction, came several times in his priestly capacity, but soon desisted, repulsed by her coldness.

Newall, to whom she turned more and more for counsel and comfort, was much with her. Unaware that she held the secret of his inner life, he talked to her sometimes of a girl "like her" whom he had once known. This invariably brought the pang that everything connected with Elinor Thornham gave her. But it served to increase her growing affection for the man whose life had been as love-lonely as her own promised to be. His encouragement tided her over the first uncertain months of her attempt at self-support ; his practical advice helped to solve the problem of daily living. At his suggestion, Liberty enlarged the kitchen-garden and added to the scanty income by selling the vegetables which he raised.

"Or perhaps, Lib," the lawyer said hesitatingly, "you and Betty may prefer to go away. In that case "—

"In the name o' Gawd, Mars Pete," interrupted Liberty indignantly, "does you *p'intedly* s'pose me an' Betty has got black insides, 'caze ou' outsides happens to be black? No, Mist' Newall, ez long ez ou' heads is hot, me an' Betty b'longs to Mars Van an' Miss Olive. *B'longs*, I say, Mars Pete! *We ain' no free-niggers!* "

"Thank you, Lib," returned Newall, grasping the huge brown hand in his and shaking it warmly.

Liberty essayed also to keep the rose-garden and the great oak-studded lawn in order. But he was soon forced to give that experiment over; and a gradual though not unlovely decay set in at Roseneath. Runners from the climbing vines sprawled over the winding walks; the grass in summer waved knee-deep where the smooth-shaven plots were wont to be, and in the winter rustled dry and yellow in the bleak wind; the rose-garden became a tangled thicket of sweets; the gates sagged, falling away from broken hinges ; the rotted roof of the old summer-house caved in, though the clambering honeysuckle mercifully hid the wreck. The house itself took on a stained and weather-beaten look. Sometimes, when her school was dismissed and Olive came down into the rose-garden to pace for a few moments its deserted paths, she seemed to herself like a ghost moving about the shadows of a long-gone but lovely past.

It was about the time her little school was opened that Olive received a letter from Duncan Jeffrey. It was in answer to one written by herself the day she and her father left Washington on their last journey to Thornham. She read it, sitting alone in the disused library ; then she came out upon the gallery where her father lay in his wheeled chair, and read it aloud to him.

For, little by little, to the sacred morning invocation, "*Father, I love you. Father, I know that you did not take Elinor Thornham's diamonds,*" — she had fallen into the habit of adding bits of the day's history ; and, finally, of telling him everything as she had been wont to do in happier days. At first the sound of her own voice, echoing as it were against a blank wall, was strange in her own ears, and the sentences would end in a hushed whisper, oftener in piteous sobs and a rain of tears. For the glazed eyes seemed still to see nothing; and the leaden face was as changeless as the face of the dead. "But he *may* hear! He may understand! Oh, father, does my voice come to you in your lonely prison? Do you hear me? Do you love me?"

And so, gradually, as has been said, she came to sit or stand by him when her day's duties were ended, or before they began; and to talk to him in a clear, low, confident tone, which often brought tears to old Betty's eyes as she listened.

"Father," she would say caressingly, "Rufe Drennon has just been here. He brought a basket of those pink lotus-lilies which grow in the lake behind Good Luck Plantation. They are lovely, all pearled with dew, and their golden stamens trembling." Or, "Do you remember Major Burnham's big bay horse, Otho, papa? Well, he has bought a perfect match for him. He drove them out this morning for us to see." Or, "Mrs. Alsbury says that her cousin, Martha Damon, whom you will remember, has come to make her a visit. She has four little girls; the oldest is named Jeanie Herring, after mamma." Or, " Liberty went down to Fair View yesterday to trim the roses on Van's grave. The flood (you know there was a flood at Fair View last spring, father, that did some damage?) does not seem to have injured our burying-ground at all."

Sometimes, in obedience to something fluttering within her, like a fledgling bird trying its wings, she half said, half sung some rhymes of her own making; or described a picture which shaped itself in her brain. Once, when she had been musing over Young Van's broken life, the tender pitying thought took shape in this wise : —

PERCY.

My little maid, whose golden hair
  Outglints the warm sunshine,
Come, round to rosy hollows fair
  Those dimpled palms of thine,
And send an elfin bugle-blast
  Across the rosy morn,
To call the bonny blue-eyed lad
  A-hoeing in the corn.

She shakes her head, the little maid;
  He is not there, she saith.

Nay then, where lush green grasses spread
  And summer holds her breath,
Mayhap he leads the loitering kine;
  Or where the sunbeams steep
The grassy slopes, and shadows dwine,
  He minds your father's sheep.

She shakes her head, the little maid;
  He is not there, she saith.
Nay then, fleet-foot and unafraid,
  He speeds across the heath,
A-chasing of the antlered deer;
  The hounds are following fair;
His ringing shout I surely hear.
  She saith, he is not there.

She brought me to the wind-swept hill,
  Whose lonesome grasses wave,
Through summer's heat and winter's chill,
  On many a heaped-up grave.
And when with trembling tongue I prayed
  The name of one who slept
Beneath the mound the newest made,
  She answered not, but wept.

Duncan's letter was dated at Paris some weeks earlier.

"I am glad you are at Roseneath," he wrote, "though I suppose you will soon be going back to the Capital. It seems far more natural to think of you in the dear old home by the riverside, than where I saw you last, in a strange city and surrounded by unfamiliar objects.

"Tell the Colonel that I fancy he will half envy me when he learns that I am on the eve of starting down into South Africa, where some genuine fighting seems to be going on. I am already tired of aimless drifting about, and if you should chance to hear of me as leading a charge either for or against some unpronounceable African chief, do not be surprised."

"Miss Olive," asked Betty, who had listened attentively to the reading, "is Mars Duncan projikin' mongs' a passel o' niggers in Affika, where Unk' Is'om Lester come from?"

"I am afraid he is," returned her mistress, laughing a little, but sighing too.

"I sholy thought little Mars Dunc had mo' 'scretion!" said Betty.

.   .   .   .

"I wonder what has become of Rose. She has not been here for more than a week."

The short winter was already beginning to break. Although there yet remained a full third of February to come, by the almanac, the air was filled with the scent of young orange-blossoms, and the elusive perfume of the sweet-olive. The sky was covered with the soft little drifting clouds which follow in the wake of a spent " norther." It was the first time for many weeks that the wheeled chair, with its heavy and dull burden, had been brought out upon the open gallery. Olive, just released from the school-room, was walking slowly up and down near it, with her hands clasped behind her, bare-headed in the soft sunshine.

Liberty, turning the brown mould with his spade in a patch beneath the library windows, was singing. His voice arose lusty and sweet on the afternoon air : —

> " 'F I 'd a wife I could n't please,
>   I 'd whop her sho 's she bawn ;
>   I 'd sen' her down to Nu Orleens,
>   An' trade her off fer co'n."

" I wonder what has become of Rose ! "

The words reached the singer, who had paused to take breath, leaning on his spade. He grunted, muttering something under his breath about " po'-white trash."

At that moment Rose herself appeared at the side-gate. She crossed the rose-garden slowly, looking over her shoulder, and stopping every now and then as if minded to go back.

As she neared the steps, however, she

broke into a little run, and reached Olive's side, breathless and smiling.

"Come into the sitting-room, Olive, dear," she whispered, with her eyes turned away from the chair and its occupant. She had never been able to bring herself to approach the half-animate thing which had been her benefactor; quivering with ill-concealed terror at the mere thought. Olive, at first deeply pained by this unreasoning and childish awe, had schooled herself into a sort of tender indulgence of it, and she now hastened to follow the trim little figure into the sitting-room. Rose drew a stool to her feet when she was seated, and perched herself daintily upon it.

"Olive," she said, blushing painfully, lifting her eyes with shy entreaty and instantly dropping them again, "I have something to tell you. I—I—hope you will not be angry. I have loved him for a long time. Oh, from the very first! Olive, I—I am going to marry Mr. Kennison."

Olive's heart gave a sudden throb; and a curious indefinable shade crossed her eyes.

"Dear Rose," she said, gathering the tearful, smiling little creature into her arms, "I am so glad. I hope you will be happy,— I am sure you will be happy."

"Do you know, Olive, darling," Rose continued, after the long and minute history of her engagement had been told, and her rapture had somewhat exhausted itself, — " do you know, I thought once — I was afraid — that Mr. Kennison loved you?"

"He never did," Olive said earnestly, " dear Rose, he never did." And she kissed again the bright upturned face.

She did not, somehow, tell her father of Rose's engagement or of her wedding. But a year later, when Big Hannah brought little Olive, Rose Kennison's baby, to Roseneath, she took the dark-eyed mite from the nurse's arms, and knelt with it beside him.

" See, papa," she said, " this is our Rose's baby — a dear little girl named for me, — Olive, Olive Kennison." She smiled a little as she uttered the name which was to have been her own. " Our Rose a minister's wife! think of it! And she is so happy. And Rufe is so proud. He has refused to live with them, though. He stays alone at the old cabin, when he is not loafing, as he has always done. He was at the back steps this morning with a bucket of honey for you, father."

XIII.

AN ARRIVAL.

It was Kennison's rejected love who pinned on the misty white veil through which his bride's face looked out at him as she floated, on her father's arm, up the aisle of St. John's Church!

Olive accompanied Rose to the church; awkward shambling Rufe Drennon stubbornly refusing to sit in the carriage with them; and there, in the familiar pew, the woman who was to have been his wife watched Mark Kennison place the golden circlet — emblem of wifehood — upon Rose's finger. Little Rose, her own friend and playmate! She kissed her when the ceremony was over, and offered him her congratulations with quiet dignity. Then she hurried back to her father.

The March wind was blowing with un-spring-like bleakness along the wide river road.

"It's as cold as a Christian," declared

June Badgett, shivering under the Man-Fig. "An' it's a mighty onlucky day for a weddin'. I reckin Rufe Drennon 'll be as biggaty as John Thornham his-se'f — marryin' his gal to a preacher."

"I sort o' thought, a little more 'n a year back," said his neighbor, "that the parson an' Miss Olive Herrin' would make a match of it. I seen 'em together ever'where."

None of the old group were left except Badgett himself, and Drennon, — at that moment hanging bashfully back from the vestry at the church, where the bridal party were signing the register. Even Dud Welsh had resigned, as it were, from the Man-Fig Council, having taken to himself a wife who had incontinently "put her foot down" on his loafings there.

"Lord," said one of the new squad, "even a preacher ain't got gall enough to marry a girl livin' under such a curse."

"What curse?" demanded another — a stranger — curiously.

"Ain't you never heerd about Van Herrin' and the Hand o' God? Well, I be dinged! Here, June, tell Joe Collop about Van " —

"Shet up," growled Badgett.

For the carriage that had conveyed the bride to the church was passing. In it, alone, leaning back, pale and thoughtful, sat Vanborough Herring's daughter. At sight of her father's old soldier-comrade, she leaned forward and bowed, an affectionate smile illuminating her beautiful features.

"Ax somebody else, ef you want to know," June continued, turning away. "I 'm plum tired o' tellin' that tale; wish my Maker may strike me stone dead ef I ain't."

. . . .

The year wore away. The vacation of the little school came and went, nothing breaking the dead monotony of the long summer days, except the visits of the few friends who remembered that Vanborough Herring still lived; and pitied, or loved, his daughter. Olive read much, sitting by the wheeled chair, often aloud, and chiefly those books from her father's library which showed his handling. By these, his favorites, she came to know him as she had never known him before, — the rare, tender, refined nature thrown back upon itself and scarce lonelier now in its torpid prison than when it had been surrounded by a world of flattering and deceitful parasites.

"Oh, had I but seen with keener eyes, and felt with a less selfish heart," she sometimes cried out, laying down her book, after reading a passage marked and annotated by his hand. And the cry shaped itself into a bit of rhyme which she often repeated : —

OH, TO LIVE MY LIFE OVER.

Oh, to live my life over!
  Not to be young again,
Not to seek peace and pleasantness
  Where I have had tears and pain!
Not for myself at all, dear Lord,
  Would I live over my life!
But I would gladly bear its woes once more,
  Its bitter wrongs, and its strife, —
If only where I have hurt my own,
  Or failed them in any wise,
I could repay them for that loss!
  If for tears in their dear eyes,
I could put smiles; if for pain
  I could give joy — O God,
I would tread the burning coals again,
  And pass again under thy rod!

One morning in the late fall she sat on the front gallery, with the invalid's chair drawn close beside her own. Betty's voice floated to her at intervals from the kitchen, where, released by a school holiday from attendance on her master, she was at work.

A letter had come from Jeffrey, — the first
for many months. It had been long delayed,
and the postmark was illegible. It was
dated, within, from a small town in the heart
of Hindostan.

" I have your letter, dear Olive [he said],
in which you tell me that the Colonel has
retired from public life on account of fail-
ing health. [This, in fact, was what she
had written some months after her father's
stroke ; she could not bear at the time to
speak more plainly ; and nothing to indicate the financial wreck had escaped her.]
I can hardly imagine him inactive, but I
am glad for your sake."

An account of various amusing and novel
experiences followed, with a description of
his present locality.

" I shall go still farther into the interior,
with my traveling companion, Ballard, who
is a capital fellow [he concluded]. Your
final and decisive answer to the question in
my letter from Cape Town makes it useless
for me to return to America. I should have
no object there except to acquire money ;

and what use has a drifting nomad like me for more money than I already possess? Only I find I cannot persuade myself to sell Good Luck. I shall hold on to that for the sake of the day — long dreamed of! — when you sat at the head of my table. My agent has my instructions, covering several years at least. And now, dear playmate, friend, sister, I must say good-by, for the guides are calling. I shall write when occasion permits, but I cannot hope to hear from you soon. God bless you. Do you remember what I told you about my uncle when I saw you last? DUNCAN."

She laid the letter — which she did not read aloud — upon her knee. Her lips quivered, and the lonely look in her eyes deepened. But making an outward gesture with her hand, as if putting something away from her, she leaned closer to the mute form beside her, and said cheerily: "The sky is so soft to-day, papa, and so blue. Away beyond Thornham, which looks as if it were asleep in the sunshine, there is a dark graying cloud that moves upward. I think it must be the smoke from the Good Luck sugar-house. The climbing sun strikes upon it, and turns its edges to silver. There is a harrow-shaped flock of wild geese just this side of it; we shall hear their *honk* presently, for they are coming this way; that means that we shall have a norther to-morrow. The river looks like liquid amber; a steamboat is going by; I can hear the hands singing on the lower deck. The road by the river-bank is like a brown crumpled ribbon."

She paused abruptly, and stood up. The big gate had swung open and two figures — a man and a woman — were advancing along the leaf-strewn avenue. The woman was Miss Kizzy. She walked with an assured tread quite in contrast with her usual hurried step. She wore the stiff and rustling black silk gown which was in general sacred to the Soirées given by the Pupils of the Jolibois Dancing-Academy to their Parents and Guardians. Her hands were gloved and a bonnet of the latest pattern crowned her head. Olive tried vainly to recognize her companion. He was small and shrunken; his knees wobbled curiously as he minced along upon a pair of very tight, very high-heeled, patent-leather shoes; a huge pair of mustachios, waxed at the ends, and suspiciously black, sprung from beneath his prominent nose, giving a grotesquely fierce look to his brown weazen face, with its small black eyes, and high cheek-bones. His dress was correct to jauntiness; he carried a cane and wore a red rose on the lappel of his coat. Miss Kizzy's hand was drawn through his arm, and he regarded her patronizingly, towering above him, from time to time.

"Olive," said Miss Kizzy, as her young friend descended the steps to meet this strangely assorted pair, "in the gentleman at my side you behold Monshur dee Jollyboys." She spoke with ill-concealed triumph. "He has returned from a highly successful Mission to the Foreign Powers. He will from this time forward reside permanently in Thornham. Monshur Anatole, this is my friend, Miss Herring."

Miss Herring stood for a moment speechless with astonishment. This shriveled and dried-up old beau the dashing hero of her childish dreams! This ridiculous figure the superb young chevalier of the Legion of Honor, whose deeds had kindled her youthful imagination! *This* the —

Monsieur de Jolibois meanwhile was bowing before her, hat in hand, so low that the bald and shiny spot on the back of his head shone at her feet.

"Thees ees an 'ona," he smirked. "I 'ave h'aspire seense thees morning to encounter Mees Eereeng. I 'ave absented myself," he explained when they were seated on the veranda, "an absence which I r-regr-ret. An' een zat absence my 'ona has suffered."

Olive started. Had he really heard of the yellow-fever patient and Miss Kizzy's flannel? And was there to be bloodshed after all?

But she was reassured, as he continued with a grandiloquent wave of his very small, very white, and bejeweled hand, "*Mais oui,* my 'ona has suffered. Madame de Jolibois has stain ze name of ze *famille* Jolibois by condescend to a School of Dance. I blame you not, *ma pauvre petite,*" he added, gallantly lifting his wife's hand and imprinting an airy kiss upon her fingers, "your Anatole knows not 'ow to cheereesh what you call *maleese.* But I 'ave remedy ze w-r-rong, Mees Eereeng; I 'ave remedy ze w-r-rong. Ze *famille* Jolibois cannot be deesgrace by a School of Dance! I 'ave open ze door to zose *enfants.* I 'ave open ze door an' deesmees zem from zat School of Dance. I 'ave told zose *enfants* zat ze vife of Anatole de Jolibois cannot no longer insult herself by conduct zat School of Dance. *C'est moi,* Anatole de Jolibois, who weell in ze future 'ave ze care of Madame de Jolibois an' ze *aimab' Zeercena!*" He slapped his stiff shirt-front and looked about him proudly.

Madame de Jolibois was regarding him with tender admiration.

"Yes, my dear Olive," she said, "Monshur *dee* Jollyboys was shocked, as I feared he would be, by my plebeian occupation. But he has forgiven me. He has dismissed the school — forever. He made a most affecting discourse to the Pupils. I think Sarah Hunter wept. You must slip away from your father, sometimes, child, and come to see us. Monshur Anatole will enter business in Thornham. But he will reserve to himself abundant leisure for less sordid pursuits."

She rose to go. Monsieur de Jolibois, after another profound obeisance to Mees Eereeng, with his hand upon his heart, extended his arm to his wife.

"I am charm' to return from my voyage," he remarked, handing her politely down the steps. "Ze village of T'ornham is vairy peetoresque; zose little hut by ze rivaire remind me of *la France.*"

Olive watched them strutting down the walk together, and then returned to her father. She related the incident to him, laughing with girlish glee.

" He looked for all the world like a Jumping-Jack," she concluded. " But no matter how he looks. If dear old Miss Kizzy is satisfied with him, that is enough. God bless her for a true and faithful friend ! "

The next afternoon, when Newall dropped in for his daily visit, he brought the news that Monsieur de Jolibois had absconded — as he termed it — again.

" History has once more repeated itself," he said. " The rascal wheedled Miss Kizzy into taking the whole of her savings from the bank, and placing them in his hands. He swaggered around all day yesterday with his wife on his arm, making calls and talking in his confounded oily way about entering business circles in Thornham. This morning he sneaked away on the train, taking with him not only all the money belonging to those two foolish old women, but the few trinkets which they possessed."

" Poor Miss Kizzy ! " exclaimed Olive, " what will she do ? "

"Do?" echoed Newall with an amused chuckle; "Madame de Jolibois, plucky, proud old soul! has already been around to see her patrons. She has explained that Monshur *dee* Jollyboys has been called away on a delicate foreign Diplomatic Mission. The sign has been replaced above her front door; and as I came by just now, Miss 'Fatty' was thumping away on the piano, and I heard Sarah Hunter's voice. The Jolibois Dancing-Academy is once more in full blast!"

.   .   .   .

The following year — the third after the awful dispensation which condemned Vanborough Herring to a living death, and his daughter to poverty and toil, there were two happenings which disturbed the unvarying quiet of Roseneath.

For Olive and her father, with the two faithful old servitors, were still at Roseneath. The times were dull and hard, and buyers of property, anywhere, were rare. Few outsiders seeking homes were attracted to the lagging old town; and these had no mind to add to the purchase-money the enormous expense for repairs necessary to the decaying old mansion and its grounds. The owner wrote occasionally to Newall, but in the main, absorbed in other things, troubled himself very little about this out-of-the-way piece of property. Olive, meanwhile, managed, out of her slender earnings, to pay a nominal rent, and when she anxiously suggested the advisability of finding another house, "Not yet," Newall invariably replied, "not yet." He well knew what a wrench it would be to her to remove her father from this sacred retreat which *in life* he had so loved. There was, besides, a secret and unconfessed pleasure to himself in seeing Elinor Thornham's kinswoman and radiant likeness flit about the house which had once been hers. And so they stayed on, Olive's school flourishing in the same sober and conservative fashion in which for above twenty-five years had flourished the Jolibois Dancing-Academy.

In the spring of that third year Kennison's young wife sickened and died. Her brief and happy married life ended quite suddenly. Two days before her death she danced like a sunbeam about the rectory-garden, calling gayly to her husband through his study-window, and showering rose-leaves upon little Olive's bright head.

The news came with a painful shock to Olive Herring.

"Dear Rose," she sobbed, standing beside the coffin in the dim church, with the two-year-old motherless child in her arms, and Rufe Drennon, sluggish in his grief as in his joy, beside her; "dear sweet little Rose! How could Death have the heart to touch your golden head! But at least your life has been happy and free of care!"

It was true. By a strange perversity of fate, the indolent, dependent, affectionate daughter of the shiftless poor-white had been shielded like a hothouse flower from every wind that blew, while the child of her powerful and aristocratic benefactor had been exposed to the merciless fury of the tempest. Poor and obscure, she had never known the pangs of poverty, or suffered for want of tender companionship. Her healthy body had rarely felt pain ; her careless heart had been untouched by grief or disappointment. Unaware of her danger to the last, she died with a ripple of infantine laughter on her lips. Putting her into the grave was like turning the mould over a bright-winged humming-bird ; or a half-blown rose whose petals are pearled with morning dew.

Thereafter, daily, like her mother before her, little Olive, in the arms of Big Hannah, came up to Roseneath. Unlike her mother the child felt no terror of the silent rigid figure on the couch, or in the wheeled chair. She nestled against it with strange confidence, lifting a tiny hand to touch the pallid cheek, or to smooth back the falling gray locks. Her first words, in a smiling effort to imitate Olive, whom she adored, were "*I wuv oo, faver, I wuv oo.*"

Following hard upon Rose's death came an incident which disturbed in many ways the tranquil if mournful life at Roseneath. Olive sat one day beside her father in the habitual gallery-nook. Rose's baby, cooing and babbling, played at her feet; Big Hannah looking on from the steps where she sat, idle and good-natured.

There was a rush of footsteps around the corner of the house, and Betty appeared, breathless, and ashen with fright.

"Oh, Miss Olive, honey," she shouted, "come quick, an' he'p me find some linen-truck fer de doctor. Lib 's done broke his laig!"

XIV.

THE DRUM-MAJOR'S LEG.

It proved to be worse than a broken leg. A tree which Liberty was engaged in cutting down in a corner of the stable-yard had toppled unexpectedly and fallen upon him, injuring his back and crushing his right leg into a bruised and quivering mass. Some passers-by, attracted by his cries, had brought him in. An immediate operation was found to be necessary, and the leg was amputated just above the knee.

The stay and prop of the forlorn little household seemed suddenly removed. For the first time since her father's affliction Olive's fortitude gave way. She bent over the rugged black face on the pillow in Betty's cabin and sobbed aloud. Feeling her tears upon his face the negro opened his eyes.

"Lawd, chile," he said, reaching out a big horny hand and patting her head tenderly, "don' cry, don' cry! I ain' much hu't.   I'm gwine to be ez spry ez ever, soon ez Doct' Alsbury gits thro' projickin' wi' my laig."

Still dazed by the chloroform, he did not know that his leg had been cut off.

This was too much for Betty, and she fled, weeping, into the yard.

The next morning, she hurried distractedly to the cabin from the great-house, where she and the young mistress together had made Herring's toilet, sorely missing Liberty's strong arms and gentle touch.   She found her husband groaning loudly, or, to speak more accurately, roaring like a wounded lion.

"Gawd-a-mighty!   What's de matter? What's de matter?" she demanded, trembling with apprehension.

"Hush, 'ooman," replied Liberty, "I'm honorin' my sickness.   Ef I don't honor my sickness, *who's gwine to honor it?*"

But this was a pretext, as he presently confessed.

"Betty," he said piteously, "in course I hates to lose my laig, an' seem-like I can't stan' de wrenchin' misery in my back.   But it ain' dat, gal, it ain' dat!   What, in de name o' Gawd, is gwine to become o' Mars

Van an' Miss Olive now? Dat chile workin' herse'f to de bone, teachin' o' dem bowdacious chillun; an' Lib a-layin' like a ole log in de bed! No mo' garden-patch! no mo' tater-patch! no mo' co'n-patch! Who gwine ter lif' Mars Van, an' dress him, an' feed him? Who gwine—*O Lawd!*"

Betty's face twitched, but she answered cheerfully.

"Don' fret yo'se'f, Lib. Big Hannah's my chile. I fotch her inter de world; an' ef she don' b'long to me I don' know who she *do* b'long to! She's mighty triflin' sence she tuck to nussin'. But she's ez strong ez a sugar-mule. I done laid down de law to Big Hannah. She's got to come fum Mist' Kennison's soon enough in de mawnin's to lif' Mars Van, an' he'p me dress him. Ef she don't I'll wear her to a frazzle!"

Liberty laughed among his pillows.

"Big Hannah's got de strenk, Betty; she got her strenk fum me. But who gwine to *feed* Big Hannah? She kin *eat* like a sugar-mule, too."

Betty soothed this anxiety as best she could, and went back to the house.

In the new order of things Olive's cares

seemed doubled. She realized more and more how she had depended upon her major-domo's great faithful heart and strong willing arms. She wished to have him removed to the house, where he would be more within reach, and less alone. But he objected.

" No, Miss Olive," he said with dignity, " I 'm better off in ou' cabin. Besides," and his eyes twinkled, " I 'd ruther be where I can honor my sickness, d'out sturbin' you an' Mars Van."

As soon as he was able to sit up in bed, he sent for one of his boys, a lad who tended Major Burnham's horses, and gave him some instructions. A day or two later Olive found the bed strewn with withes of white-oak. Liberty, propped up among his pillows, was weaving baskets to sell.

Meanwhile there was quite a little flutter among Liberty's white friends, for his patient and unselfish devotion to his former owner in his misfortunes had won him many. This was no less than a project, originating with Madame de Jolibois, to buy him an artificial leg.

" One in the very latest style," Miss Kizzy explained to Newall, sitting in his office.

"I learned from Sarah Hunter, whose uncle-in-law lost his limb at the Battle of Shiloh," she went on, "that for a sum which I confess seems large, Peter, these artificial limbs may be procured in the North. I am at present in correspondence with a firm in Philadelphia. In fact, I am negotiating for a second-hand limb" —

"Second-hand!" gasped Newall.

"Second - hand," repeated Miss Kizzy firmly. "The limb, which corresponds to Liberty Thornham's proportions, was made, it appears, for a drum-major who lost his limb in a battle during our war. I do not know what battle, for I regret to say that the drum-major was in the Yankee army. I feel that I ought to offer an apology to the people of Thornham for having decided upon buying — if the money can be raised — a limb which has been worn by one of our enemies. But being second-hand (for the drum-major, they inform me, returned it after using it about a year), — *being* second-hand, I get it at half-price."

"How much money have you on hand?" Newall asked, taking out his purse.

"The fund, Peter, amounts as yet to only a few dollars," she returned. "But several people have promised to subscribe, and there will be mite-meetings, in Mrs. Alsbury's yard and elsewhere, for the benefit of the fund. Were it not for the unavoidable expense of Monshur *dee* Jollyboys' trip I could do more myself. Liberty has been informed of this movement. But of course we do not wish Olive to know as yet," she added anxiously.

"You are a good woman, Keziah," Newall said, doubling his subscription, which he could ill afford at the moment, "and if ever a man in this world has done his duty, that man is Lib Thornham."

Madame de Jolibois went away radiant. The fund under her indefatigable generalship grew; but it grew slowly. Sixty dollars was a large sum to raise for such a purpose; and it was a full year before the drum-major's leg came, consigned to Madame de Jolibois.

Long before this Liberty had contrived a pair of crutches strong enough to bear his immense weight.

"I kin werry along wi' dese ontell I git de dum-major's laig," he said to Betty, regarding them with just pride.

He swung himself on them to the great-

house every morning to superintend his
master's toilet. Big Hannah and her
charge arrived promptly from the rectory
at the same hour. Kennison, in his untidy
and silent home, was pleased to have his
child under Miss Herring's guardianship.

Big Hannah's duties in the sick-room
completed, with what assistance he could
give, Liberty then assumed charge of the
invalid and the child; seating himself in a
split-bottomed chair brought over from the
cabin, and setting about his basket-weaving;
while his daughter, obediently though not
with alacrity, trudged out into the garden-
patch.

"Neb' mine, Miss Olive," he said in answer to the expostulations of his mistress,
" neb' mine ; Mist' Kennison 'hiahs Big
Hannah to nuss his chile. Big Hannah 's a
mighty po' nuss. I kin tek keer o' de chile
a heap better 'n *she* kin. At de same
time Big Hannah ain' los' her *laig*, an' she
kin drive a spade an' han'l a hoe better 'n
I kin. Ef I kin nuss better 'n Big Hannah, Mist' Kennison ain' got no call to complain ! "

" But how about Big Hannah ? " his mistress asked.

"Lawd, Miss Olive, Big Hannah ain' complainin'! But ef she dassen to open her mouth, her mammy's got strenk 'nuff to wear her to a frazzle!"

The long-expected leg arrived at last. Doctor Alsbury fetched the box over in his buggy and assisted at the unpacking. Liberty examined the straps and buckles with staring eyes, and hugged the somewhat battered leg (the drum-major had evidently been in the habit of using it as a projectile!) to his bosom with loud hallelujahs. But he broke down and cried like a child when he found that he could not wear it, try as he would.

"Hit ain' no use, Miss Olive," he said dejectedly. "Dat dum-major's laig don' seem to fit, no matter how me an' Betty ties an' onties dem strops. Seem-like dat Yankee dum-major has *hoodooed* dat laig, anyhow!"

He stood it up against the foot of the four-post bed in his cabin, regarding it with a mixture of awe and admiration as he went in and out; and occasionally he tried it on.

"Dem Philadelphy folks ain' got much jedgment, nohow," he finally concluded, philosophically whittling out a new crutch.

XV.

No prison is without a door, and sooner or later, in one way or another, every captive escapes from bondage.

So it was at last with Vanborough Herring.

The time was spring, — a little more than five years from the day the soul was thrust into its donjon-cell. His daughter was standing beside him; Rose's child was pattering about the sunny gallery; Liberty sat on the steps with his crutches beside him watching Big Hannah spade the lettuce-bed below; the voices of the school-children at their noon play on the front lawn blended pleasantly with the plantation hymn Betty was singing over her wash-tubs.

"Do you know, father," Olive was saying lightly, "I had a curious dream last night. I thought I saw mother and Van come across the rose-garden hand in hand. They called to me, and I ran out to where they were.

And all at once we were all back in the
"other house," and you had little Jeanie in
your arms. And then "—she paused and
stooped to kiss his forehead, but started
back with a cry. A quiver was running
along his limbs; his ashen face was purpling. Oh, God in Heaven, was it life coming back?

No, not life! Death had opened the door,
and the prisoner was free!

The daughter's grief was terrible. It was
utterly incomprehensible to those who for
years had been saying to each other how
much better for him, and for her, if he could
only die; even Newall wondered at it. Only
Betty, gathering her nursling in her arms
and weeping with her, could understand the
sudden void, the aching loneliness in the
heart throbbing so painfully against her
own.

"Yes, honey," she said soothingly, "Maum
knows. It's like losin' a baby. My ole
arms is achin' yit a'ter my fust little gal, an'
she been onder groun' mo' 'n thirty year."

"If he could have spoken to me,—just
once before he left me, Maum Betty! If he
could have given me one look! If he could
only have known *truly* that I did not be-

lieve "— And here there was an added pang, which Betty's mother-heart — knowing nothing — yet dimly divined. She pressed the tear-stained face closer to her bosom.

"Ez to *knowin'*, honey," she whispered, "don' trebble 'bout dat; Mars Van knowed it all 'fo' he went. Ef he did n' he sholy knows it all now."

He looked, lying in his coffin, with the quiet majesty of death upon his marble face, — the face which had settled back into the beautiful and regular outlines so well re-membered by those who knew him best, — he looked as if he might in truth know all. The smile hovering about the closed lips was one of triumph.

"*A Vanborough! Impossible!*" John Thornham's hot words leaped back into Newall's mind as he stood looking down upon the dead man.

"Impossible, indeed," he murmured. "Whatever secret Vanborough Herring is carrying to his grave, it is not one of dis-honor!"

They buried him in the Thornham family burying-ground at Fair View. The shadow of the stone at Young Van's head fell athwart the grave as they lowered the casket beside the mouldering coffins, already placed there, of his wife and two little children.

It was not the Rector of St. John's who read the burial-service over the dead, but Father Dalton, the superannuated old Methodist preacher, who had known him when he was a little lad in Kentucky. He recalled this fact in his homely and familiar discourse, and spoke at some length of certain traits of character in the boy which had developed nobly in the man; he dwelt upon the kindness and generosity which had always distinguished him as a friend and as a citizen; and referred to his secret benefactions,—and at this some among his listeners winced.

"And now, my brethren," concluded the old man, looking somewhat sternly around upon the large crowd of people, who from various motives had followed the dead man to his last resting-place, "I say unto you, beware lest in your foolish judgment you mistake the wisdom of the Almighty. Whom He *loveth* He chasteneth. A blessing oftentimes hath the outer shape and disfigurement of a curse. Was not the Hand of God heavy also upon his servant Job?"

The sun had set, and the sudden shadows of nightfall descended even as he spoke. In the hush that followed his words, the outer circle of hearers, — the negroes who had once called Vanborough Herring master, — gathered together under Liberty's leadership, broke into a mournful hymn, which yet had in its refrain a ringing undercurrent of exultation : —

> "I traveled fur an' I traveled fas',
>   *Mo'nin', O good Lawd, mo'nin'.*
> Night-time come an' I drapped at las',
>   *Mo'nin', O good Lawd, mo'nin'.*
> Now in de mawnin' I open my eyes —
>   *Shoutin', O good Lawd, shoutin'* —
> In de shiny mountains o' Paradise ;
>   *Shoutin', O good Lawd, shoutin'.*"

.   .   .   .

"I would like to remain a few days longer at Roseneath," Olive said, talking over her plans later with Newall. For the time was indeed come when she must leave Roseneath.

He nodded abstractedly. It was plain that his thoughts were elsewhere.

"Of course I shall keep my school," she continued, "not only for my own support and that of dear faithful Maum Betty and Lib, but to save me from utter loneliness."

"Olive," said her companion abruptly, "have I not by this time something like a father's right to take care of you?"

"Dear friend," she replied, pressing her lips to his hand which she held in hers, "you have always the right to love me, and advise me, and comfort me. Nay, more," and she smiled a little wistfully up into his face, "you have the right to scold me, too, whenever you like. But a great healthy young woman like myself to sit quietly down to be taken care of! For shame, Mr. Peter Newall! You should not encourage such idleness."

"Well, my dear," he sighed, disappointed, "it must be as you wish, I suppose. But I have your promise to come to me when you need anything. Certainly you must stay on here as long as you wish. It will take some time to set the smaller house we have rented in order. But I fear you will be very lonely."

She was lonely. Yet, as the long summer days drifted by and the time approached for the inevitable change, — the dismantling of the old familiar rooms, the gathering together of personal belongings, the removal to a strange house, — she clung more and more, with a frightened sort of feeling, to the very loneliness and desolation about her.

.   .   .   .

Kennison was sitting beside his study-table. The August noontide was stiflingly hot; the lifeless air in the small room was heavy with the perfume of the cape jessamines in the garden outside, — the perfume which always reminded him of Rose's coffin, which had been smothered under them. He pushed back his chair impatiently and threw down his pen, leaning back at the same time to draw the dingy curtains across the open window.

The Rector of St. John's was looking gaunt and worn. He was barely thirty years of age, but he had long lost all semblance of youth. People said it was the climate and the death of his young wife. His dark eyes were strangely sunken; his hair was quite gray; there were deep wrinkles on his forehead and around the drooping corners of his mouth. His sad and overwearied air was in harmony with the lonely shabbiness of his surroundings. During the two years of his widowhood things had gone pretty much as they pleased at the rectory; now the older women of the congregation were beginning to say that the rector ought to look about him for a "suitable" mother for his child.

He got up and walked listlessly to the door. There was a rattle of wheels in the street, which ceased abruptly; and Doctor Alsbury called from the gate, —

"Good-day, parson. I brought your mail over, — a couple of letters and some newspapers."

"Thank you, Alsbury." He came out and stood by the buggy.

"You look fagged out, Mr. Kennison," continued the doctor. "Jump in and drive about with me a little. It is pretty hot, but the open air will do you good. I am going down to Rufe Drennon's ca — house. He's been laid up for a week and I have not seen him since the day before yesterday."

"What is the matter?" asked Kennison.

If Rufe Drennon had not been the rector's father-in-law, the doctor would probably have characterized the attack as "pure laziness;" as it was, however, he replied carelessly, —

"Oh, nothing in particular; seems to be a little feverish, and complains of headache. He'll pull up in a day or two."

Kennison called Big Hannah, — for, for once in a way, little Olive and her nurse had elected to spend a part of the day at home, — and gave her some directions. Then he stepped into the buggy and they turned down the dusty but well-shaded lane that led to the outskirts of the town.

Drennon's cabin stood in the midst of a small field which at present was a tangle of sunflowers and cockle-burrs. It was built of logs, and in its day and time had been a comfortable dwelling-place. There were two rooms, with a wide open passage-way between them, and a couple of shed-rooms in the rear. But the chimney, straining away from the end wall, seemed on the eve of tumbling to the ground; the roof drooped under the weight of rotting shingles; the floor of the passage-way was broken in many places; it looked as shiftless and dilapidated as Drennon himself.

They found him lying on an unkempt bed in one of the shed-rooms. There seemed to be no one else on the premises. A pitcher of water was set on the floor within his reach; an ill-smelling lamp on a shelf above the head of the bed was still burning, its flame looking strangely forlorn in the sunlight which streamed in through the open door.

The moment the doctor's practiced eye fell upon his patient, his countenance changed; his careless expression gave place to grave anxiety. He laid his hand on the brown hairy wrist stretched along the soiled coverlet and felt the pulse. Drennon looked at him with dull curiosity.

"Well, Doc," he said in a husky whisper, "I reckin my time's come, ain't it?"

The physician did not reply; he was hastily mixing some brandy and water in a cracked teacup.

"Swallow this, Rufe," he said, slipping his arm under the pillow, and lifting the sick man's shoulders.

But Drennon moved his head aside fretfully.

"'Tain't no use, Doc," he said, "my time's come. I've had innard fever off 'n' on fer mo' 'n six months; an' sence I've been layin' here, I've felt somep'n snap som'ers inside me. An' I don' keer. I'm plum tired anyhow. I never did keer much," he rambled on, his voice now stronger, now sinking into a faint monotone, "cep'n fer Rosy; Rosy's things is all in them two front rooms. She fixed 'em up herse'f, — them two front rooms. I ain' never onsettled 'em sence she lef'."

Kennison looked at the doctor, who had seated himself on the side of the bed after forcing a swallow of brandy down Drennon's throat, and was softly chafing one of his hands.

"What does it mean?" he asked in an undertone.

Alsbury shook his head.

"Death," he replied briefly. "A sudden collapse. There is no possible hope. He is dying."

"I know it," said Drennon, opening his eyes, for he had sunk into an uneasy slumber; "an' I don't keer. But afore I die I want to tell about them di'mon's."

"What diamonds?" demanded Alsbury, warning Kennison with a glance not to speak.

"It was this-a-way, Doc," continued the sick man with a slight show of eagerness. "I useter sell things to Miss Elinor, — you *know*, — fresh eggs, an' blackberries, an' figs, an' sech. An' that night I tuk a basket o' figs to Rosencath, 'cause I heerd she'd been a-honin' a'ter figs. I went late, 'cause Rosy was afeerd to stay by herse'f, an' I had to wait ontell she was asleep, — po' little Rosy!"

"Well?" said the doctor, again motioning to Kennison to keep out of sight.

"Well, I come 'crost the rose-gyarden without seein' a soul, an' I started to go roun' to the front do'. But all at onct, I heerd Van Herrin's voice inside, an' I crope back an' tuk off my shoes, an' went up on the side-gall'ry to the winder. He was in the settin'-room with Miss Elinor. They had done quit talkin' an' he was standin' by her. She was a-layin' on the lounge. I reckin he was tellin' her good-by. They useter be sweethearts, Miss Elinor an' Van. He started to go an' she called him back an' showed him a box. I seen her open it. He took it an' looked at somep'n inside it. Then he laid it down on the table, an' stooped over an' kissed her onct. Then he opened the blind, an' come out'n the winder, an' jumped down fum the gall'ry, an' went 'crost to the rose-gyarden gate. Ef he had looked 'roun', he might of seen me. But he did n't. I heerd June Badgett hollerin' to them mules of his'n out in the road, an' I waited ontell he got by; an' then I knocked on the winder, an' went in with my basket. I wa'n't thinkin' o' nothin' but sellin' them figs an' gittin' back to Rosy. But Miss Elinor's eyes were shet; an' I seen she was asleep. She wa'n't dead; she was sleepin' like a baby. I would n't of done it ef she had been dead. That box was layin' where Van Herrin' had put it, an' I took it an' put it in my pocket, an' crope back, an' got my shoes, an' come home. An' nex' mornin' I heerd that Miss Elinor was dead."

Kennison could restrain himself no longer.

"What!" he thundered, "*you* were the thief! *You* took those diamonds! and all these years you have allowed an innocent man to suffer for your crime!"

"You neenter holler so loud, parson," said Drennon peevishly. "I ain't deef."

"For Heaven's sake, Mr. Kennison," urged the doctor, "be quiet. The man is sinking rapidly. Let him finish his story."

As he spoke, he put the brandy and water again to his patient's lips.

"I don' want no medicine, Doc," whispered Drennon. "Don't you be skeered. I ain't goin' to die ontell I git good an' ready! Ef the law had a-tuk up the case, I'd of come forrard quick enough. Or ef Johnny Thornham had of prosecuted, I would n't of let the law tech him. But I knowed no Thornham wa'n't goin' to prosecute no other Thornham! Onct I had 'em in my pocket when I tuk Mis' Herrin' some truck she ast me to git her out'n the woods. But I did n't git no chance to give 'em to her. An' when she tuk Rosy an' was so good to her, I did n' dassen to give 'em to her, less'n she 'd turn Rosy out. *I* did n' want 'em. They wa'n't no manner o' use to me. When Van Herrin' was struck, Doc, I kep' tellin' that fool June Badgett not to be so blame shore about the Hand o' God! When Van got struck I useter take Miss Olive ever' nice thing I got a holt of — peaches, an' honey, an' eggs, an' flowers. I did n' want no pay fer 'em. But she would n' take nothin' without pay. Them Thornhams is mighty biggaty! Anyhow, I never spent none o' that money. I 've got it all — ever' blame cent."

He felt feebly under his pillow and brought out a little blue calico bag, and emptied its contents — a handful of silver dimes and quarter-dollars — on the coverlet.

" Ever' cent Mis' Herrin' ever give me, an' ever' cent Miss Olive ever give me; Doc, I want you to give it to Miss Olive."

"I will, Rufe," said Alsbury. "But what became of the diamonds, Rufe? Have you got them?"

"Yes, I've got 'em. I've jest had to keep 'em. *I* did n' want 'em. The Lord knows they wa'n't no good to me. But I had to keep 'em. I useter lock 'em in the cupboard, but I fetched 'em to bed with me yistiddy, because I knowed my time had come. An' I don't keer. Tek 'em, Doc. An' that's all I got to say."

The dying man felt under the pillow again and thrust into the doctor's hand a small leather case; then closed his eyes, and turned upon the pillow as if addressing himself to sleep. He did, in fact, fall asleep almost instantly, breathing at first heavily, then more softly, and finally, flutteringly, and at long intervals. Doctor Alsbury, with the little jewel-box in one hand, and the other upon the sleeping man's wrist, sat perfectly silent for a long time; the shaft of sunlight that fell across the floor receded steadily; the breeze freshened a little; the afternoon was waning. At length he leaned forward with a sigh and drew the covering over the haggard face on the pillow.

"He is dead," he said gently.   "Poor Rufe!"

Kennison, who sat stunned and motionless in a corner,—all thought of his calling clean gone out of his mind,—looked up at the sound of his voice; then arose and came forward, staggering like a drunken man. The doctor also arose, opening, as he did so, the little casket. It contained an old-fashioned necklet,—a slender thread of twisted·gold; the heart-shaped pendant that hung upon it was set with two or three small and insignificant stones. On a yellowed slip of paper in the box were the words, "*For little Olive*," in a woman's handwriting.

A spasm distorted Kennison's pale face— of rage against the dull clod, forever beyond his reach, lying at peace upon the sordid bed? Of shame at the recollection of his own cowardice? Of self-pity? He could not himself have defined the feeling which overwhelmed him. He took the box from Alsbury's hands, and looked at it.

"*Elinor Thornham's diamonds!*"   The words burst from him in a hot resistless flood. "The priceless necklet!" he sneered.

"Priceless indeed! An honorable name for its sake dragged in the mire; an innocent man hounded to his grave; a happy family destroyed! Ay, and more, by Heaven! A young and tender creature tortured by a coward — a brute" —

He checked himself suddenly and rushed from the cabin, and across the field to where the horse and buggy had been left in the shade of a live-oak. Untying the lines with mad haste, he sprang into the buggy and drove away, deaf to the amazed halloo of the doctor, who stood in the door of the cabin, gazing after him, apprehensive for his reason. He drove furiously, lashing the old horse into a foam, until he reached Roseneath.

There he alighted and walked rapidly across the grounds, and entered the house by the familiar side-hall. Olive was in the little sitting-room. She sat by the window with her hands folded idly in her lap, and her dreamy eyes turned toward the garden. At the sound of footsteps she looked up.

Kennison was standing, wild-eyed and haggard, on the threshold.

"Miss Herring," he said, in a loud unnatural voice, "I wish—I must speak with you."

She sprang to her feet.

"Little Olive! Oh, what has happened to her?" she cried, growing pale.

"The child is well," he returned, advancing until he stood directly in front of her. "It is not of little Olive that I have to speak." He faced her a moment in silence as if trying to collect his thoughts, then he went on: "I have this moment come from the death-bed of Rose's father—of Rufus Drennon, my father-in-law. No, do not interrupt me," he said, as she made a gesture of sympathy.

"Miss Herring—Olive—the last time I was in this room I stood where I now stand, and told you the story of your father's crime—wait," for she had drawn herself up proudly, and was pointing to the door,—"wait, I beseech you, and hear me out. I told you what people were saying of his disgrace and his shame. I told you that I thought it my duty, as a servant before God's altar, to break the troth which hardly twenty-four hours earlier I had plighted to you. I told you that I could not ally myself with a family upon which such a stain

rested; I could not marry a woman whose
father was a criminal though unpunished;
a thief though free from the clutches of the
law. Wait, I beg of you! I told you all
this, standing where I now stand, and looking, as I now look, in the face of your father's
daughter. Well, I come to you, now, to
tell you that I — the proud, the virtuous,
the lofty-minded man and minister of God,
who would not contaminate himself by taking in his your innocent white hand; I, the
despicable coward; I — Mark Kennison —
I married the daughter of the real thief;
my wife was the child of the man who stole
Elinor Thornham's diamonds."

Olive, who had listened, spell-bound, re-
coiled at the last words.

"What do you mean?" she gasped, pale
to the very lips. "What do you mean?"

She almost shrieked the words, catching
him unconsciously by the wrists.

"I mean" — he spoke more slowly, for
he was beginning to feel weak and exhausted — "I mean that your father lived
and died an innocent man — unjustly ac-
cused, foully slandered. I mean that Rufus
Drennon, my wife's father, has confessed
with his dying breath that it was he who

committed the crime for which your father has been branded in this community for nearly twenty years " —

He caught her in his arms; for the room whirled about her, and she could no longer stand. Her white glorified face rested a moment on his breast.

" O God, I thank Thee ! " she murmured in ecstasy. " *Father, Father !* "

He waited until the flow of happy tears allowed her again to listen. Then, word for word, he took up the story as Drennon had told it; as it had burnt itself into his brain ! His lips were dry and parched and his tongue almost refused to obey his will as he repeated mechanically the uncouth phrases of the dying man.

" Oh," she cried, putting out a hand to stay him, " in pity do not tell me any more ! It is enough for me to know that my father's honor is vindicated."

" I must," he groaned, " I must ! "

And when he had finished, he took the paltry casket from his breast-pocket, and laid it on the table beside her. Then he went away.

She snatched up the box as soon as he had left her, and ran out into the yard, crying : —

"Liberty! *Liberty!* Maum Betty, where are you?"

"What in de name o' Gawd is de matter wi' de chile!" said the old man, sitting up in bed; for he was resting his tired back. "Soun's like she got somep'n on her min'!"

"No it don't!" cried Betty, running to the door, "it soun's like she 's got religion! What is it, honey?"

Olive, panting and happy, threw herself into her nurse's outstretched arms; then she flew to the bedside.

"O Liberty," she sobbed, "it was not true! It was never true! I knew he never could have done it! O *father! father!*"

The old people stared at each other, mystified. She poured out the glad tidings, laughing and crying in the same breath.

"And after all," she concluded, "the necklet was mine! My cousin Elinor must have intended him to take it away with him! See, Maum, here is my name on the card — *for little Olive.*"

"Lawd, is *dem* de di'mon's dat made all de splutter*ment?*" asked Lib, contemptuously eying the old-fashioned ornament. "Hmp! Ef Mars Van been in de *way* o' stealin', he sholy would ha' tuk somep'n better 'n dem glass beads! Yes, chile, I has always knowed dat monsus lie 'bout Mars Van — me an' Betty bofe. I mashed de mouth o' de free-nigger dat had de insu'ance to tell us! In cose, Miss Olive, I knowed Mars Van was wi' Miss Elinor dat night, 'caze I tuk de note to his office axin' him to come. She tole me to keep de yuthers out'n de way. Seem-like she sort o' shame to let anybody but me know dat she saunt fer Mars Van. Anyhow, when all dat human-cry riz up 'bout dem di'mon's, I kep' my mouth shet. 'Caze I knowed Mars Van had been wi' Miss Elinor. *An' ef Betty's Marster wanted to tote off a passel o' di'mon's, I —* Oh, in cose I knowed he did n't *do* it, honey! I knowed he did n't *do* it! An' dis is de fus' time I has even tole dat *I* knowed Mars Van was at Roseneath dat night!"

"Ez fer Rufe Drennon," remarked Betty, "what kin you 'spec' fum po'-white folks, anyhow."

Olive returned to the house, walking on air; her heart sang like a freed bird. As she passed around the vine-hung nook of the gallery where the dumb and motionless invalid had so often lain in his chair, she stopped.

"*Ah, Sir Lancelot, there thou liest,*" — the words rose involuntarily to her lips, — "*thou that wert never matched of earthly knight's hand; and thou wert the courtliest knight that ever bare shield; and thou wert the truest friend to thy lover that ever bestrode horse*" —

She sought her memory in vain for the next sentence; and she turned into the library. The little squat copy of "Morte d'Arthur," how well she remembered it! It used to be always in Young Van's hands. She went to a small bookcase in a corner and began searching among the books that had belonged to her brother. Yes, there it was, with its battered binding and torn leaves!

"*And thou wert the kindest man that ever strake with sword; and thou wert the goodliest person that ever came among press of knights.*"

She closed the book and laid it back on the shelf. "Yes, you were all that and more, my father, my hero!"

She was turning away when something wedged in between a couple of volumes on the same shelf caught her eye. A confused sense of recognition stirred her at sight of it, and she took it down. It was a somewhat bulky diary, bound in red morocco. Some letters were fastened to it with a bit of tape. She turned it over in her hands; the confused memory became clear in a flash. It was the packet which she had seen her father thrust into his pocket as he came out to her on the gallery that last fatal afternoon — the day his voice had ceased forever in the midst of his life-story! She now remembered seeing it lying on the floor after Liberty had carried him into his room. Some one had doubtless picked it up, amid the excitement, and placed it in the cabinet, where all these years it had remained unnoticed and forgotten. This surmise was correct, Job afterward admitting that it was himself who had "lef' it dar, ontell Mars Van mout ax fer it," and then forgotten it.

The packet was marked in her father's bold handwriting: "*Private and Personal.*" Olive untied the tape with shaking fingers and examined its contents.

There were several letters; some of these were quite yellow with age. One was from Herring's mother, written evidently when

he was a little boy and away from home for
the first time. The grand-daughter smiled
a little at the old-fashioned phraseology;
but the tears sprang to her eyes as she read
the *post scriptum :* —

And above All things, my Son, you must
be Honest and Faithful, and Never break
your Word, though you should be Reviled
for keeping it.   MOTHER.

Two letters she laid aside as too sacred
for even a daughter's eyes to dwell upon;
they were marked: " *From my beloved
wife.*" Besides these there were one from
herself, — a funny little scrawl; she remembered quite well the day she wrote it,
and sent it in one of her mother's to the far-
away camp in Virginia ! — and one in Young
Van's sprawly schoolboy hand. Another
was indorsed on the envelope, " *John Thornham. Received Oct.* 14, 1857."
Olive unfolded the large business-looking
sheet. The letter, dated from New Orleans,
began abruptly : —

VANBOROUGH HERRING : I do not know
what wrongs my sister Elinor suffered at

your hands, or what stain you may have placed upon the old and honorable name you bear. I do not wish to know. My sister evidently cherished for you until the day of her death a feeling which her wrongs — if she had any — had been unable to destroy. I find among the papers which I brought away with me from Roseneath a letter addressed to myself, written shortly before her death, and intended to be read, as it has been, after she had passed away. It was her wish that certain property belonging exclusively to herself should be converted into money and given to you unconditionally. Or rather, with the sole condition that the gift should remain a secret between you and myself. You may have some idea concerning her reasons for this condition; I have not. At any rate, I make no doubt — whatever your character may be — you will respect her wishes in this matter. But I will be greatly obliged if you will affix your name to the inclosed line attesting under oath your intention of submitting to the above-mentioned condition. Upon receipt of this, the money, amounting to fifty thousand dollars, will be placed in the bank of ——— in Galveston subject to your demand.

I desire also, with your permission, to add to this the sum of one thousand dollars for the purchase of the negro, Liberty, who belonged to my sister Elinor, to belong in future to your daughter, Olive Vanborough Herring; named, as I understand, for my mother. With this proviso: that she be kept in ignorance of her ownership of this piece of property until she is twenty-one years of age. If anything in this latter transaction strikes you as strange, set it down to the well-known eccentricity of the Thornhams.

Let me hear from you as soon as possible.

JOHN THORNHAM.

Some further correspondence had evidently passed between the two men relative to these bequests: for there was another letter, undated, but written probably some weeks later. It was very brief : —

I am glad to know the truth, so far as you are concerned. I could not bring myself to believe that a Vanborough could be guilty of a thing so dishonorable. Take the money, then, with a free heart, as she wished, poor girl ! But bear in mind the condition which she herself imposed. Your little Olive resembles my mother strangely.   J. T.

On the margin of this note was the memorandum: — "*J. T. died of yellow fever in New Orleans in* 1859."
To these letters, clearing the mystery of Herring's sudden acquisition of money for the purchase of Roseneath and other property, his daughter did not attach the significance which they assumed in the eyes of Newall when he examined them later. The main fact — Drennon's confession, which removed the stain of infamy from her father's name — made all else seem of small importance. A dim recollection of a tall dark man bending over her and softly repeating her name, *Olive Vanborough*, flitted intangibly through her mind as she read the lines which concerned the gift to herself of " the negro, Liberty." But she was too absorbed to grasp it.
She laid aside the letters and took up, reverently, the leather-covered diary. Its closely written pages contained the story — much more in detail, and brought to something like a conclusion — that her father had partly related to her. It was begun in

Washington, evidently soon after Duncan's visit; but appearances indicated that the last lines were written the day of their arrival at Roseneath.

It was a passionate outpouring of the man's inmost soul; penned perhaps as a relief to the repressed and tortured life; certainly meant to be overlooked by no human eye save his own. Olive quivered as she read; fascinated, stirred, shaken to the very depths of her being by the spectacle of a great tender heart, bare and bleeding under her gaze.

"She told me," the narrative went on, after describing at some length that part of the writer's interview with Elinor Thornham which related to the broken engagement and her reasons therefor, "she told me that she wished me to have the property which had come to her, personally, from her grandmother, who was also mine, and which was absolutely at her own disposition. She did not mention the amount; and at that time I supposed it to be trifling. For reasons which at this distance of time I shrink from putting upon paper, I at first and with some warmth declined this legacy. But her agitation at my refusal was so extreme that, alarmed by her suffering, I promised to do whatever she wished in all matters. 'One of these days, then,' she said, 'I hope you will live at Roseneath.' This remark I hardly noticed at the moment; she was very weak and ill, and my thoughts were more upon herself than upon what she was saying. Finally, she opened the little casket, which she had held during the whole of our interview in her hand, and showed me a necklet — a child's gewgaw — which she had worn when she was my Olive's age, desiring me to send my little daughter to her the next day, that she might clasp it around her neck with her own hands. Then, at last, I kissed her an eternal good-by, and came away. She seemed so nervously anxious lest my presence there should become known to the inmates of the house that I passed out at one of the windows, and crossed the rose-garden to the gate. I saw no one, though I seem sometimes, when I recall it all, to have heard the sound of wheels in the road outside."

An account followed of the circumstances of Elinor Thornham's death and burial; and of John Thornham's first letter, and of the narrator's surprise at its contents.

" I did not understand the full meaning of Thornham's reference to Elinor's wrongs," he continued ; " at that time I supposed him to allude only to the broken engagement and to my subsequent marriage. I felt justified in writing him a full account of my last interview with his sister, wherein she explained her motives in severing those early bonds, and of my own conduct in consequence of her (supposed) unjust and wayward treatment.

" I thought I understood Elinor's wish to confine the knowledge of her bequest to her brother and myself. She had, in fact, in her last talk with me, hinted that my wife might very naturally be disturbed by such a legacy from the woman whom I had once loved. I stated this frankly. I could not, I said, for the sake of the money, give pain to the mother of my children. Some money due me in Kentucky from a family lawsuit, and about to be paid, would, as he suggested later, — and did, — render any explanation to my wife unnecessary. I did not, unhappily, take the outside world into account. In referring to John Thornham's own gift to my little girl, I mentioned Elinor's legacy to her of the neck-chain, a circumstance so trivial in itself that but for his peculiar interest in the child I should hardly have remembered it at all. I now know that this disposed, for him, of the hideous charge which, unknown to myself alone, had been brought against me by the people among whom I lived; while in his reference to it I read simply enough an allusion to the broken engagement. So, after a somewhat prolonged correspondence, I signed the written condition."

The writer gave a minute account of his journey to Galveston, where he received the money which he brought back to Thornham, and which he at once invested in the purchase of Roseneath, and in laying the foundation for later speculations. He described the growing and inexplicable coldness of many of his neighbors and friends. This at first, absorbed in arranging and planning for his new ⋆life, he scarcely noted; then, — his overwhelming astonishment and indignation when by a curious chance he learned the cause.

"I doubt whether in that moment," he wrote, "stung to the heart's core by this calumny, I should have justified myself even if I could honorably have done so. In regard to the theft of the necklet, indeed, which seemed as ridiculous as it was unjust, I could have made no explanation whatever. I did not know, and I have never been able to conjecture, what became of it, unless some servant entered the room and took it after I left her and before the others came in to find her dead on the couch. Curiously enough, no one — except possibly a few friends foolish enough to believe in me — ever seems to have given me the benefit of this doubt. I found myself suddenly surrounded by a horrible atmosphere of suspicion and distrust. No word was ever spoken openly in my hearing, no chance given me to cram the lie down the throat of my slanderers. I said to myself, foolishly enough, that Truth is mighty and will prevail; and I waited."

Olive's horror and indignation deepened as she read on. It was all there; the mute questioning in the eyes of the wife; the daily torture of the sensitive, shrinking boy; the slowly hardening pride of the strong man, conscious of his own integrity; the quickly destroyed illusion of hope which was born of the soldier's gallant record; the defiant despair which followed the death

of his first-born; of his wife and little children.

"But Olive, at least, — my bright sunny-
hearted Olive, — had never been made to
share or bear this awful burden. By a miracle for which I thanked God daily, on my
knees, she had escaped all knowledge of
the cloud which hung over us. But at
last " —

The last pages, burning with a record of
his anguish upon learning that his cherished
and adored daughter had at length been told
the infamous story, were written more hurriedly than the rest. These were doubtless
the pages that he had penned that last day,
and just before — impelled by some forever
unknowable feeling — he had partly broken
the seal of silence. The almost illegible
characters and the confused ending of the
sentences, showed that, even as he wrote,
the unseen enemy was creeping upon him.

As the daughter, with tear-reddened eyes,
finished reading the last pathetic words:
" *For myself, I no longer care, but for
Olive,*" — a step sounded on the gallery.

"Oh, Mr. Newall!" she cried, springing
up and running eagerly to meet the lawyer,
" have you heard? Do you know? "

"Yes, I know!" he responded, almost choked with emotion; "I have just seen Alsbury. Poor Van! And that scoundrel, that villain, Rufe Drennon" —

"Oh," she interrupted, "he is lying yonder in his cabin, dead. Rose's father, little Olive's grandfather! Let us not think of him, poor ignorant Rufe! Think rather of how my father must be rejoicing where he is, at sight of my happiness!"

She placed the diary and John Thornham's letters in his hands.

"Think of my chancing upon them this day of all others!" she said, showing him their hiding-place.

His eyes lighted as he glanced through them.

"I at least am bound by no vow of secrecy, Olive, my child," he said when he had finished. He rose and took his hat. "And before I sleep to-night all questions concerning your father's life, so far as a prying public has any right to ask, shall be fully and forever answered."

He lingered only long enough to explain the significance of the documents he held.

"Here come Doctor and Mrs. Alsbury, Major Burnham and his wife, and Jack

Addington," he called back from the door. "Let them rejoice with you, Olive. They have the right, as true and faithful friends of your father."

"Come back a minute, Mr. Newall!" She met him as he turned, and placed her hands on his shoulders. "I know who has been the truest and faithfulest of all," she said, looking affectionately at him, "and if a daughter's love and devotion can re-pay"—

"Repay! nonsense!" he interrupted with a gruffness belied by his beaming face; "who dares to talk of payment of any sort between father and daughter!"

XVI.

THE storm which had raged in Kennison's soul seemed to have spent itself when he left Olive Herring shedding tears of sacred joy over the vindication of her father's good name, and came out once more into the open air. He walked slowly down the wide avenue, and, passing out at the park-gate, entered the road which led townward, wholly forgetful of Alsbury's old horse which stretched a long neck toward him from the rose-garden wicket, whinnying and tugging at the hitch-rein.

He felt bruised and sore, as if he had come out of a sharp physical contest. He wondered dully at his late outburst, well knowing that nothing could ever move him again. He tried vainly to recall the scene in Drennon's cabin. A blurred picture only, in which he himself had no part, presented itself to his mind, — a shaggy head turning restlessly on a pillow; a belt of sunshine lying across an uneven floor; a line of small ants crawling up the leg of a rickety table, — and the fragmentary vision faded away. Finally he ceased to think altogether, moving automatically along the dusty highway without volition of his own. But something startled him suddenly again into life. It was the voice of June Badgett calling to him from the Man-Fig, where he stood with his back against the gnarled tree-trunk.

"Hello, parson," he drawled, "wher have you been? You look like you've seen a ghos'."

Kennison ran forward and stopped, facing him savagely. The demoniac fury which had possessed him came surging back with increased violence. His breast heaved; his white lips quivered in an impotent attempt at speech. He was seized with an insane desire to smite the old man in the face; his clenched fist trembled at his side as he hissed, at length, rather than said: —

"Do you want to know where I have been, June Badgett? Well, I will tell you. I come from the death-bed of the man who stole Elinor Thornham's diamonds."

There was a movement of curiosity among the idlers lounging around. Badgett started forward with an inarticulate cry; his eye-balls seeming ready to burst from his head.

"Diamonds!" Kennison stopped and laughed scornfully,—"a miserable little trinket, too insignificant to buy even *your* soul, June Badgett, contemptible as that is!"

"Who was the thief?" ventured one of the crowd, unable longer to contain his curiosity.

"The thief?" echoed the minister. "The thief," he said with deliberate slowness, "was one of your own friends, and my father-in-law, Rufus Drennon."

And without noticing the amazed ejaculations which arose about him, he told the story again, as he had a little while before told it to Olive Herring, using Drennon's own words, and unconsciously copying the dying man's very gestures and intonations.

"And there," he concluded harshly, addressing Badgett, "there is where I have been, and that is the ghost I have seen."

With that he turned abruptly and continued his walk toward the village.

The effect of this revelation upon Badgett was terrible.

"*I done it. God-a-mighty, I done it!*"

he shrieked, throwing up his arms and clutching wildly at his gray hair.

Nobody ever stopped to think of it, but June had nearly reached the allotted three-score and ten of years; his once burly figure was bent and shuffling; his flabby face was seamed with wrinkles, his eyes bleared and sunken.

"Jedge not that ye be not jedged," he continued hoarsely. "I thought Van took 'em. I wish my Maker may strike me stone dead ef I wa'n't shore that Van took 'em! ' I done all the mischief. I done it! I kep' the parson fum marryin' the sweetes' young gal in Thornham! I done it all! God-a-mighty let jedgment fall on me! Let the Hand o' God strike ole June Badgett, an' strike hard. God-a-mighty have mercy on my soul. I done it!"

His companions fell back, staring at him in helpless wonder, and finally slunk away, one by one, leaving him alone under the Man-Fig.

.   .   .   .

As Kennison approached the village he saw Doctor Alsbury standing in the midst of an excited group, gesticulating and talking loudly and rapidly. For the first time

he remembered the horse and buggy, and
half turned, wondering idly how Alsbury
had got to town. But the torpor was on
him again, and he plodded on, heavily, toward his own house. The group about the
doctor was breaking up; people were hurrying away to tell the news; heads were thrust
out of office windows; horsemen were leaning from their saddles; the air was thrilled
with breathless questions and excited re-
plies; women came running, bareheaded, to
their gates, calling to each other and to
chance passers; they shrank aside, frightened, as Kennison stumbled by with staring
but unseeing eyes.

He reached his study at last, and threw
himself into a chair, where he sat motionless
and without thought or feeling, for hours.
A summons to supper failed to rouse him,
though he had eaten nothing since morning.
Big Hannah lighted the lamp, looking at
him curiously, for she had already been up
to Roseneath to talk over the wonderful
news and to ask Miss Olive whether she
should put " mo'nin' " on little Olive for
her grandfather; she withdrew silently, for-
bearing to intrude even his child upon her
stricken master.

As the hours passed, the lonely man became aware that something was beginning to pierce through his apathy — something strangely, poignantly sweet. He felt upon his breast the nestling touch of the head that had rested there for one brief moment that day. A thrill passed through him and he arose, instantly alert and alive. The shame and the disgrace were forgotten.

"Oh," he cried in a sort of ecstasy, "she will surely understand when I tell her how it has all been a dream — a strange, sad, terrible dream, which began in this very room the night when, coward and fool that I was! I cast her out of my life, and with her all that was best and highest within me! Surely she will understand! Has she not kept herself free all these years? Can it have been for my sake? Olive, Olive, all that has been dead so long — poetry, romance, feeling, the desire to achieve, the longing to do — all that mates with your own high and ardent soul — is reborn within me at this hour! Together — together we will " —

He paused, exhausted with excess of emotion. A lingering smile illuminated his pale features. He arose and passed into the next room, where his child lay sleeping in her crib, Big Hannah nodding on the floor beside her. He stooped and kissed the red slightly parted lips, and as he did so his heart smote him, remembering her mother.

"Dear little Rose," he murmured, " you at least were innocent and loving. But I do no wrong to your memory, Rose, for you loved *her* always; yes," he whispered, " I will go to her to-morrow morning. She will understand. Olive, *Olive Kennison*," he smiled, bending again over the sleeping child.

He forced himself to remember, as he turned away, that he would be compelled the next morning to make arrangements for Rufe Drennon's funeral.

" But I will not let the day pass without seeing her—Olive, my Olive," he said impatiently, throwing himself, without undressing, upon his bed.

XVII.

A SUMMER AFTERNOON.

OLIVE HERRING arose early the morning following the confession and death of Drennon. She had lain awake — for very joy! — the short summer night through. But she felt no fatigue; she ran like a child about the old home, now become dearer than ever; and along the brier-grown walks of the garden.

"Oh, if he could only have lived to this day!" she cried at last, seating herself on the step of Betty's cabin, and looking up in her nurse's sympathetic old face. "If they could have all shared this happiness — father and mother and Van! Think what it would have meant to them, Maum Betty, after all they suffered."

"Dass so," said Betty, "but don' you fret yo'se'f, Miss Olive, chile. Dey kin see an' onderstan'. An' dey sholy is shoutin' in Kingdom-Come dis minit!"

Soon after breakfast, people began to

drop in upon one pretext or another. Some of these visitors were old friends; many were mere acquaintances; but all came, interested and congratulatory. It appeared that no one in Thornham had believed the slander, after all!

Newall's lip curled a little cynically, as he watched the procession stream in and out, and listened to the buzz of reminiscent indignation. But there was no room for bitterness in Olive's soul. She met her guests with frankly extended hands, her heart throbbing with exultation.

" How good they all are ! " she said to herself again and again. " Oh, if he were but here beside me, my father ! "

Toward noon, when everybody had gone, even Newall, who was as restless as a lover away from this daughter of his heart, she went up into her old bedroom, unused these many years. The flat air was musty within and the purple shadows lay heavy along the floor. She moved softly forward, and her blood tingled; for she seemed as she entered to catch an elusive glimpse of her mother's white-robed figure, stealing away from the bedside, where she had so often knelt to pray above her sleeping child!

She opened the door of the huge cedar *armoire* which stood in an alcove.

"How foolish I am!" she exclaimed, rummaging among its contents; "and yet, why should I not, on this wonderful day?"

She chose from among the heap of half-forgotten garments laid away on the sweet-smelling shelves the diaphanous rose-pink gown which she had worn that long-gone summer afternoon when Kennison had breathed into her ears the old-new story whose end was heartache and bitterness. She slipped it on, fastening the dainty ribbons and smoothing the yellowed laces into place. Then she walked to the long mirror, lifting the skirts from the dust.

"How foolish I am!" she repeated. "Why, I am past twenty-five. I am a dreary old maid!"

The face looking back at her from the glass belied her words. It was a marvelously beautiful face. The troubles and anxieties of these later years had but added a subtler charm to the lovely features, a more luminous depth to the dark eyes. She smiled at the slightly old-fashioned look of the gown which sheathed her slender figure, exquisite in the virginal purity of its outlines ; the smile made the mirrored face so radiantly young that she started back, wondering if that could indeed be herself! Hastily loosening her abundant and beautiful hair, she wound it in the old way about her head, letting the curling tendrils caress her white neck and lie on the low white brow, — from which every trace of mistrust had vanished. Then she stood with a finger on her lip, smiling bashfully, as if half-ashamed of her own loveliness.

"Miss Olive," said Big Hannah, appearing in the doorway holding little Olive by the hand. The child dashed forward, screaming with delight; a black sash was tied about her waist, and the sleeves of her white gown were fastened with black ribbons. Olive blushed guiltily ; she had forgotten Rufe Drennon's funeral!

" Lawd, Miss Olive, how pretty you does look ! " cried Big Hannah, her eyes wandering in open and undisguised admiration over the daintily arrayed figure before her. Then, recollecting her errand, " There 's a gent'lum downstairs waitin' to see you, Miss Olive."

There was a significance in Big Hannah's voice which brought the blood to the cheek of her mistress.

"A gentleman? Very well, Big Hannah. You may say that I will be down in a few moments."

She hurriedly unfastened the ribbons of her gown, but retied them after a second's consideration.

"No," she murmured, "I will not take it off. On this day, at least, I will wear no mourning."

She descended the long flight of steps slowly. Her heart was beating fast. She was beginning to shrink painfully from the interview which she had instinctively foreseen.

On the landing she turned, irresolute; then with sudden determination she ran swiftly down and entered the little sitting-room. There was no one there. Puzzled, she crossed the wide hall to the drawing-room.

The curtainless windows were open, and a drowsy breeze, drifting in, stirred the faint perfume that arose from the tall spice-jars in the chimney-corners. She stood for a moment on the threshold, the bare polished floor reflecting the rosy cloud of her draperies. Then with a single rapturous cry she flew into his arms. There was no greeting, no question, no answer. Her face was on his breast; her tear-wet eyes were shining into his; his caressing inarticulate words were in her ears; his kisses were on her lips, her cheeks, her hair!

" When — when did you come?" she asked, when at last she found voice to speak.

" Just now," returned Duncan. For it was Duncan Jeffrey — a little stouter, and very bronzed by his tropical wanderings, but young, erect, and handsomer than ever. "Just now; I drove out direct from the station. Old Dud Welsh came over on the train with me from H——. He told me — O Olive, how could you *dare* not to tell me?" he broke off reproachfully.

" He told you" — she urged breathlessly.

" He told me of your father's — affliction and death. And of the loss of the money; and of your school. O Olive, how brave, how noble you have been; and what a blundering, ignorant, selfish fool I have been! How can you ever forgive me! How can I ever forgive myself for loitering aimlessly about the world, as I have been doing all these years, leaving you to" —

"Duncan," she interrupted earnestly, "have you seen no one? Have you heard nothing else?"

"Why no," he replied. "Jack Addington ran out and hailed me as I passed the warehouse, but I did not stop. Why? What? Olive" — a sudden alarm shook his voice, — "what more is there to tell? You are not — Good God, Olive! You are not married?"

She extricated herself from his arms, half-vexed, half-laughing.

"No, I am not married. But, Duncan," her voice quivered a little, "tell me. Did you know the story of my cousin Elinor Thornham's diamonds when you asked me, six years ago, to marry you?"

Jeffrey blushed scarlet through his sun-burn and tan. But he answered promptly, "Yes, I have always known it."

He waited, afraid to add another word.

"And did you think that my father carried away — that my father stole those diamonds?"

"*Olive!*" he cried, recoiling.

"Did you?" she persisted, gazing steadily at him.

"I don't know," he said, flushing again,

and painfully embarrassed. "I only know that I always thought him the bravest, noblest, and truest gentleman that ever lived. But if he had been a thousand times over what they said he was, how could that have made any difference in my love for you? I would still have wanted you for my wife if every drop of blood in your body had been akin to a race of thieves and murderers."

"Oh, I am so glad!" she cried, clinging to him hysterically. "I almost *hoped* that you believed it!"

He looked at her wonderingly, not daring in his unhoped-for happiness to ask a question.

"I will tell you everything presently," she said, answering the look, "but first, about yourself?"

"Oh, myself!" he echoed scornfully, drawing her to a sofa and seating himself beside her. "I am out of all patience with myself. And yet, Olive, your letters were so placid and cheerful. I had no hint from any one else. The letters from my agent — a newcomer in Thornham, you know — contained simply business details, and were very rare at that. I have been tramping about strange countries, wearying myself with strange peoples, and trying to keep myself from remembering too much and longing too much.   That is about all. One night, nearly four months ago, lying in a lonely camp in Ceylon, under the shadow of a ruined temple, with no one near me but my native guides, — for Ballard came home long ago, — I seemed all at once to hear you calling me.   I did not wait for daylight. Within the hour my face was set Westward. I have been telling myself daily ever since that I was an idiot to come with *that hope.* And I had almost persuaded myself that I was hurrying back because I was homesick for the smell of the sugar-boiling at Good Luck.   Now " —

He stopped to lift her hand to his lips.

" But Olive, dear," he continued, " why did you let me go away?   Why have you kept me away from you all these years, if you " —

" If I loved you? " she finished the sentence for him frankly.   " I did love you, Duncan," she went on, looking bravely in his face, though her cheeks paled and her voice shook. " I have loved you always; yes, even when for a little while I was under the spell of Mark Kennison's poetic and highly strung nature. Even at the moment of plighting my troth to him the thought of you stirred me so strangely that I forced myself to put it aside."

This confession from the lips of the woman loved so long and so hopelessly was almost more than the eager listener could bear. He leaned forward, gazing at her with adoring eyes, no longer caring to know why she had held him away from her. In this supreme moment, the weary years behind him were forgotten; the despair, the heart-ache, the self-torture — all had fallen away like an outworn garment!

"Yes, I have always loved you," she repeated dreamily. "But I dared not let you marry me after — I wish to tell you everything, Duncan. Listen."

He listened, breathless, while she related all that had passed between Kennison and herself that summer, six years ago; the wooing in the old summer-house; the intervening day, with its bright and joyous memories of her father; the final and terrible rupture. She spared the minister as much as possible, softening his language to herself, and hurrying over his statement of the public belief in her father's guilt.

But in the midst of the recital Jeffrey started up, the veins on his forehead swollen with anger.

"The scoundrel!" he shouted, "the cowardly contemptible scoundrel. I will" —

"Do not blame him too much, Duncan," she said gently. "Remember, he was a stranger here then. Since that time, he has had more to suffer than you yet know. Besides" — an arch smile curved her lips.

"Besides, God bless him!" Jeffrey exclaimed, seizing her hands again and covering them with kisses; "besides, if he had not been such a contemptible coward, perhaps I should not be the happiest man in the universe to-day!"

"Perhaps," she assented, still smiling. "Then you came back," she said, taking up the thread of her story again, after recounting the meeting with her father and the then inexplicable change in his open attitude toward her. "Even in the midst of the shame and agony which overwhelmed me when he — Kennison — left me that day, Duncan, the thought of you, and how differently you would have acted, came to me to help me and comfort me. But how could I let you take into your life one upon whom rested such dishonor and disgrace that another man, plighted to her by sacred vows, had deemed it his duty to abandon her?"

" Do you mean to say, Olive," demanded Jeffrey almost sternly, "that this was the reason you refused to be my wife?"

" This was the reason, then and after," she replied simply. "Was it not enough? I told myself that perhaps you, like myself, had never heard the story; that you did not know of the horrible suspicion that clung to us — of the dark blot upon our name. More than that, oh Duncan!" she burst into a fit of passionate weeping, "there were times when I think I must have believed it myself!"

" No, you did not," he said, soothing her, "you never did. Poor little girl!"

His tone and the touch of his hand on her bowed head reminded her of her father; her tears flowed afresh but more quietly.

" It was the same when you came to us in Washington," she went on when she had grown calm once more. " The thought of your going filled me with sadness, and a sort of terror which seemed to forebode some coming evil, — as indeed it did! But I could not, I dared not, link to yours a stained and dishonored name. I think that my father understood this feeling, though, knowing of my broken engagement, and divining its cause, he may have thought that my heart clung to that lost illusion. But he loved you as his own son, Duncan. If he can look upon us now, I know that he is happy at seeing us united at last."

"For all time, please God," interrupted Jeffrey solemnly.

"For all time! Dear father! Those were happy months in spite of all — that winter at Washington! — I saw him so admired, so honored, everywhere — for the first time really himself: open, genial, gay. And I saw into the secretest recesses of his soul — except the one place where he kept in honor, and for the sake of a pledge given to a woman's memory, the secret which had ruined his life."

She dwelt long and tenderly on the home-coming and on the half-finished revelation made the same day by Herring. The stroke of paralysis; the sudden shattering of the fortune so rapidly amassed; the long patient weary years which followed — of all this she spoke less freely; the wounds were too recent, the soreness too great, in spite of the ecstasy of the past twenty-four hours.

" Kennison married Rose ! " Jeffrey exclaimed at that point of the narrative. " I cannot conceive of it ! Yet she was a pretty, clinging, warm-hearted little creature. And has she been happy with him ? "

" She died three years ago. Yes, she was happy. Dear Rose ! You must see her little girl, Duncan, a little girl named for me — Olive ; Olive Kennison."

Duncan reddened angrily, then laughed at the absurdity of his jealous thought.

Then came the history of Drennon's illness and death. The all but incredible story of the theft produced upon Jeffrey an effect as electrical as it had upon Olive herself. He walked about the room in a transport of joyful excitement, hardly able to contain himself.

" Did you not say," he asked curiously, when the long and absorbing recital was finally concluded, and they sat hand in hand, silent from the very fullness of content, — " did you not say that Kennison married Rose Drennon ? "

" Yes."

"Then he became the son-in-law of the actual "—

"Don't, Duncan," she implored, laying her hand on his lips. "Let us forget that forever. Let the dead rest in peace; and as for the living — what I have myself suf‐ fered makes me tender toward the pain and mortification of Mark Kennison."

"Provided it is only that!" he returned, smiling.

"And now, Duncan, you will understand what I meant when I said that I almost hoped you believed the story of my father's crime when you asked me to be your wife. Another man had cast me away from him because of it. You, in spite of it "—

"Hush!" he said peremptorily. "I will not have it. I forbid you ever to refer to that again. Do not my own sufferings for the past six years count for something?"

"O Duncan!" she threw herself into his arms again.

At that moment, Betty's voice rang through the house.

"O Miss Olive! Fer Gawd's sake! Hally‐ hally-*lu-jah!* Glory! De fountain o' bless‐ in' keeps a-runnin'! De Lawd's name be praise'. Amen!"

She appeared in the doorway, her turban on one side, her suds-wet hands clasped above her head, her eyes streaming.

"What is it, Maum?" cried Olive, flying to her.

"Lib! Miss Olive, Lib! He's stompin' 'roun' on de dum-major's laig same ez ef he ain' never los' his'n. He's been practicin' onbeknowns to me, an' he's done stropped it on by his-se'f, dat dum-major's laig; an', bless Gawd, he's a-struttin' 'roun' de back-yard like a peacock! He's feered to come up de steps, less'n he slip down — why, Mars Dune, is dat you?"

"Yes, Aunt Betty, I have come home to stay," he replied, coming forward and grasping her hand.

"Hmp," she grunted, "it wuz high time!"

"I think so myself, Aunt Betty," he said. "I have been a fool to keep away all these years."

"I agrees wi' you, Mars Dune," she admitted candidly.

Liberty's stentorian voice calling obstreperously, "Betty! Betty! where is you, gal?" recalled her to the business in hand, and she hurried out.

"Go and see him, Duncan, dear old Lib!" Olive said. "I will join you presently."

She ran into the little morning-room. Here, where so many dark hours had descended upon her, she wished for a moment to be alone with her sunshine.

.   .   .   .

"She mus' be in the settin'-room then," said Big Hannah outside; and Madame de Jolibois entered, accompanied by Miss Serena. Both were clad in deep though eccentric and Dibbs-like mourning.

"Be not affrighted at these habiliments of woe, Olive," said Miss Kizzy, embracing her quite cheerfully. "You have before you the widow and the sister-in-law of the late Monshur *dee* Jollyboys. Death has bereft us of our natural protector. Yes, Olive, Monshur Anatole expired a year ago in his native land. I received the information of his demise the day before yesterday. Hence these funereal trappings. And hence the reason of Monshur Anatole's failure to return to enter business and social circles in Thornham. I feel as a wife; Serena feels as a sister-in-law. We shall wear these outward symbols of grief forever."

"Oh, I am so sorry," exclaimed Olive, conscious on a sudden of her pink frock and ribbons.

"I sorrow at not having been with him in his last moments," continued Miss Kizzy; "so does Serena."

Miss "Fatty," smiling and comfortable on the sofa, nodded assent.

"Pray forgive my appearance, Miss Kizzy," Olive hastened to say. "I put on this colored gown because — of course you have heard that my father's honor has been vindicated by" —

"Dear child," interrupted Madame de Jolibois, "I am delighted to see you in your present attire. Such raiment is appropriate to your youth and beauty. As to Vanborough Herring, he needed no vindication in my eyes. I never doubted him."

"I know you never did, dear, dear friend," cried Olive, throwing her arms about the withered neck.

She started up. Kennison had entered silently, and stood looking down at her. His face showed traces of the painful struggle of the previous day, and of the night's sleepless vigil. His hands shook, he looked ill and worn, but there was a light in his eyes which had long been a stranger to them.

Olive read in his nervous and hesitating manner his disappointment at not finding her alone. She covered her own embarrassment with a cordial welcome, and was talking on indifferent matters when Jeffrey entered with Liberty, proud and happy on, the drum-major's leg. Betty, radiant, followed, carrying the crutches in case of accident.

"Hello, Kennison!" cried the returned wanderer with a heartiness whose genuineness surprised himself. The sight of his forlorn and defeated adversary stirred his generous nature to the quick.

Kennison started and stammered; but, instantly recovering himself, he took the proffered hand in his own.

"I am glad to see you back, Jeffrey," he said, "when did you arrive?"

"I declare, Miss Kizzy!" Duncan said, when he had answered a volley of questions from everybody, including Newall, who had hastened back to Roseneath as soon as business would permit, "I do declare you look younger than you did the day you stood me in a corner for declining to *dosy-do,* as we

used to call it, with Kitty Washington!
And how goes the Dancing-Academy?"

Madame de Jolibois tried hard to recover
the tone of decorous woe which she had
thought fit to assume.

"I do not, Duncan," she replied, "consider it proper that the relict and the sister-
in-law of a *dee* Jollyboys should continue to
degrade his memory by teaching the Saltatory Art, and I have concluded an arrange-
ment whereby Sarah Ann Hunter shall
henceforth and forever conduct the exercises
in her own name, and receive all the emolu-
ments. We have rented our mansion to her.
It will in future be known as the Dibbs
Dancing-Academy. I am somewhat apprehensive concerning the future of the very
young ladies and gentlemen of Thornham,
but Sarah Ann Hunter has our example before her eyes, and I trust she will continue
to feel the solemn responsibility of her position. Serena and I will retire to private
life. That is, we shall take in sewing for
our maintenance."

"You will do nothing of the kind, Miss
Kizzy," Jeffrey said warmly. "You and
Miss Fa — Miss Serena will come and live
at Good Luck — with us."

He glanced at Olive as he spoke.

"Ah!" cried Newall, delighted, "then that is what fetched you home, you young rascal!"

"The hope of it brought me," Duncan said frankly.

Kennison's pale cheek grew a shade paler.

Olive had opened her lips to declare boldly in the face of them all that her betrothed when he spoke knew nothing whatever of Drennon's disclosure. But seeing the pain and chagrin in the rector's eyes, she forbore.

"Yes," Jeffrey was saying, "we shall keep Good Luck, and spend a part at least of each year there. For the rest, our plans are hardly made as yet, except that we shall be married within the month — from Roseneath."

"Why, Duncan!" remonstrated Olive, forgetting in her surprise that they were not alone, "you know that not a word has been said about" —

— "From Roseneath," continued Jeffrey calmly. "And we may run over to the other side for a wedding-trip. Olive needs a change of air."

" Ef Mars Dunc had a-humped his-se'f dat-a-way six year back," muttered Betty in an aside to Liberty, " he neenter gone foolin' 'roun' Affika, an' he neenter waited nuther ! "

" Dass so," said Liberty in the same tone, " but den, 'oomans an' gals is dat onsartain dat mebby ef he *had n't* a-gone to Affika, an' been so bowdacious long a-comin' back, de chile might n't o' *had* him ! "

" Dass so," grinned his wife.

Jeffrey, pushing a chair aside, dislodged something from the little table. It fell to the floor; he stooped and picked up the rusty leather box which contained Elinor Thornham's " diamonds."

" What is this?" he asked carelessly.

Olive reached out a hand and took it from him.

" It is nothing," she said quietly, putting it out of sight, — " a forgotten plaything."

Kennison, turning to go, gave her a grateful look.